The compassion and willingness to understand that she saw in Sam's eyes gave Nora a courage she'd never dreamed she had. For the first time in her life, she dared proceed on a wing and a prayer.

"I want to know firsthand what all the books and movies and songs are about."

"And you think I can show you that?"

She nodded.

"Nora, cabin fever can play games with your emotions, and you just ran away from the altar," Sam reasoned. She didn't want reason.

"My marriage would have been nothing more than a business arrangement. I'm tired of doing everything by the book," she said with conviction. "Don't you see? I want to experience one wild, crazy, madly passionate, maybe even ill-conceived love affair. I don't want this chance to pass me by.... And I was really hoping you wouldn't, either."

Sam folded Nora into his strong, warm embrace. "Like I could refuse you after a proposal like that."

Dear Reader,

During the eighteen years my husband and I and the kids lived in Austin, Texas, it snowed only twice—and melted the next day in both cases. So you can imagine our excitement our first winter in North Carolina, when we learned a major snowstorm was on the way. Unfortunately we couldn't have been less prepared. We had no rock salt or sand for the sidewalks, no shovel to clear them and perilously few supplies.

Gamely, we ran out to get milk, bread and a bag of rock salt. (We didn't get a shovel because we didn't really think we'd need one.) We put our eldest daughter on a plane back to college. And settled in for a few inches.

The "few inches" turned into the Blizzard of '96—delivered in three separate back-to-back storms that closed schools and businesses for a week. During that time, as my family and I struggled to dig our way out of the driveway with a garden shovel, a hoe, a rake and other assorted garden tools, I found myself doing plenty of daydreaming. What if a runaway bride, a schoolteacher on a fieldtrip and a young mother with her baby got stranded by the snowstorm, at the worst possible times, in the best possible places, with the men of their dreams? The result: Three new romantic comedies—*Snowbound Bride*, *Hot Chocolate Honeymoon* and *Snow Baby*.

I hope you enjoy reading all three books in my new trilogy, BRIDES, BABIES & BLIZZARDS, as much as I enjoyed writing them.

Best wishes,

Cathy Gillen Thacker

(who now has two shovels and a bag of rock salt, "just in case.")

Cathy Gillen Thacker

SNOWBOUND BRIDE

Harlequin Books

TORONTO • NEW YORK • LONDON
AMSTERDAM • PARIS • SYDNEY • HAMBURG
STOCKHOLM • ATHENS • TOKYO • MILAN
MADRID • WARSAW • BUDAPEST • AUCKLAND

ISBN 0-373-16713-X

SNOWBOUND BRIDE

Copyright © 1998 by Cathy Gillen Thacker.

Chapter One

"I can't believe we're going to get hit with the snow-storm of the century, today of all days, when Gus is bringing his bride-to-be home to meet us!" seventy-four-year-old Clara Whittaker said, worry etching her face.

Sam Whittaker watched as his grandmother rushed around before going off to work at the family-owned department store, putting her spotless country kitchen in order.

"Now, Gran. I'm sure Gus'll make it to Clover Creek intact," he reassured her. "Though as for his bringing a woman..." Sam paused, not sure how to put this, only knowing he didn't want to break his hopelessly romantic grandmother's heart. "Gus didn't exactly say he was getting married, you know. Only that he had a surprise that was going to be *presented* to all of us around three or four o'clock this afternoon." He held up a hand, effectively silencing his grandmother before she relayed her concerns. "And again, you've no reason to worry. Storm or no storm, I'm sure Gus's surprise'll be here."

Sam only hoped Gus didn't break any laws this time. The situation with the borrowed Humvee, the

Santa, the faux reindeer and the damaged parking meters during the Christmas holidays had been a little sticky. At least until Gus had agreed to pay for all damages, in lieu of the citation and fine Sam had had no choice but to impose.

"Well, I don't know what the rest of you think, but I know what Gus said and what he didn't say, and I *still* think he's bringing home a bride," Clara said emphatically as she strode to the bay window to look out at the pale gray storm clouds obscuring the early-morning sun.

"You may have a point," Harold Whittaker murmured thoughtfully as he brought out galoshes for himself and his wife. "Gus always said he was going to be married by the time he was thirty-five. He's been hinting at a satisfying new romance in his life for weeks now. Not to mention debated—in theory only, of course—the virtues of having a wedding right here in Clover Creek, West Virginia, as opposed to the more metropolitan New York City. *And,* let's not forget, his thirty-fifth birthday is Saturday."

"The only question is how is Gus planning to introduce the woman of his dreams," Sam's seventeen-and-a-half-year-old sister, Kimberlee, said as she, too, cast a glance at the wintry gray sky before gathering her book bag, coat, earmuffs and gloves into her arms. She swept the length of her long golden-brown hair over her shoulder, away from her face. "You know Gus would never do it in any *normal* way."

"That's the understatement of the year." Sam thought about his older brother's penchant for distinctly unforgettable fanfare as he chugged the last of his coffee. He noticed the first intermittent snowflakes starting to float down from the sky. The white specks were almost too tiny and far apart to even be called flurries, but they were a definite harbinger of the storm to come. They looked so peaceful and delicate, serene, even. Hard to believe the weather forecasters expected the seemingly harmless flakes to whip up an all-out wicked winter blizzard. As a law officer, he'd have his hands full in a few hours. And so would everyone else up and down the East Coast, although the storm would likely wreak havoc differently in each locale. Some cities would lose electricity. Others would be inundated with ice and sleet, as well as snow. Unlucky travelers would get stranded—probably in the worst possible place, at the worst possible time. And school would be cancelled everywhere.

Mentally shaking himself, Sam turned back to his grandparents and sister. "Clover Creek still hasn't gotten over Gus's parachuting onto Main Street when he arrived for that impromptu visit last fall," he recalled. Never mind the two minor auto accidents and the painting mishap caused by his unheralded descent from the sky. And that day, Gus had had nothing in particular to announce to the world, save his unannounced homecoming. Sam didn't want to imagine what spectacle Gus would decide a *wedding* needed.

Clara smiled and shook her head. "That grandson of ours always knew how to get attention, even before he became as rich and famous as his celebrity clients." Clara slid the rest of the breakfast dishes into the dishwasher and looked at Sam. "You know, Sam, you ought to take a page from your brother's book and snag yourself a bride, too.''

Sam rolled his eyes at his grandmother's match-making tendencies and leaned over to slide his own coffee cup into the machine. He'd only been back in West Virginia for a year and a half. During that time, his grandmother had fixed him up more times than he could count. Always against his will and without his knowledge. And always with poor results. He'd been hoping she'd eventually cease and desist. *Not a chance.*

Gran continued to counsel him. ''You're not getting any younger.''

''I'm thirty. Hardly a candidate for the bachelor hall of fame,'' Sam murmured, moving closer to the space-saving television set mounted underneath the kitchen cabinet.

''You'd never know that to hear the ladies around here talk!'' Kimberlee teased as Sam strained to hear the latest weather report coming from the TV. He frowned, realizing it did not look good. They were predicting two to three *feet* of snow across the entire Eastern Seaboard, from South Carolina to Maine, and in some places, ice and sleet. ''They say there hasn't been a woman around here who's held your interest for more than five seconds yet!'' Kimberlee continued, in a voice that was both amazed and impressed.

Sam shrugged, his gaze focused on the weather map. Right now, the radar map showed the storm moving slowly over the southernmost tip of South Carolina. It wasn't predicted to hit West Virginia full force until much later in the day, which meant they still had hours to get the local emergency management forces—most of whom were volunteers—ready.

"When the chemistry's right, I'll know it," Sam replied distractedly, switching the set off with a decisive click.

Impatient to get to work and do what needed to be done, he buttoned the top button of his starched khaki shirt and knotted his regulation black tie.

"Until then, why waste each other's time, pretending it might amount to something, when I already know in here—" Sam paused to thump his chest over his heart "—it won't?"

Sam's grandparents and sister exchanged skeptical looks as they, too, prepared to head off to work and school.

"I know what I want when it comes to a woman," Sam continued as he pinned his name tag and silver badge that proclaimed him sheriff of Clover Creek on his shirt. The four of them pulled on their coats in unison and headed out the door of the rambling old Victorian home to their cars.

"When—" *and if,* he added uncomfortably to himself "—I find my Ms. Right, I won't let her go."

"I would hope not," his grandfather murmured, opening the door of their four-wheel-drive minivan for Sam's grandmother.

Sam wanted the same kind of enduring, loving relationship his parents had had while they were still alive. The kind his grandparents still did. He wanted all the sacred vows offered. A marriage that nothing and no one could tear asunder.

"Until then, I've got a job to do," Sam said determinedly, casting another look at the fine, sparse flakes falling from the sky above.

And he knew that would not be any easier than finding a mate would be. As the chief law enforcement officer in a growing but predominantly rural area of West Virginia, filled with serenity-seeking yuppies, young families looking for a great place to raise their kids, senior citizens looking for a great place to retire and original residents, also known as "country folk," he would have his hands full attending to whatever calamities the storm engendered.

Sam's heartbeat picked up, and he grinned, already anticipating the challenges ahead. Whatever the next few days and the snowstorm of the century brought, Sam had a feeling it would definitely *not* be easy, and it would definitely not be dull.

NORA KINGSLEY couldn't believe it. It was starting to snow outside, with—she'd just heard moments ago on the car radio—what was being dubbed as the snowstorm of the century on its way. If she knew her overbearing father and equally controlling ex-fiancé, she probably had half the law enforcement officials along the Eastern seaboard on the lookout for her by now. And, worst of all, she was *stuck* in this darn dress! No matter what she did, the zipper on her wedding gown was not moving up, and it was not moving down. And that left her literally trapped in the exquisite floor-length confection of satin and lace.

Giving up on the frozen zipper of her off-the-shoulder gown with a groan, Nora picked up her skirts, moved to the sink and took stock of herself in the mirror. She had absolutely no lipstick left on her lips. Her heart-shaped face was flushed humiliation pink and streaked with the remnants of her tears. Her dark brown hair was a curling, windswept mess. Of course, it was no surprise that she was a wreck, Nora thought disparagingly, as she quickly washed her face and blotted it dry with a tissue from the dispenser. It had been one heck of a day and, sad to say, at only two in the afternoon, it was far from over yet.

Not that she should be surprised about that, either, Nora thought as she smoothed on moisturizer and lip gloss to protect her face from the bitterly cold winter air outside and then quickly redid her makeup.

She'd known from the get-go that she shouldn't marry someone she'd liked and known forever but wasn't entirely sure she loved. Yet she'd foolishly allowed herself to be talked into it by her father and fiancé anyway. Only to find out fifteen minutes before the ceremony was to begin, when she inadvertently stumbled onto a secret pre-wedding meeting between her father and Geoffrey, that Geoff had stood to gain more than just a wife from the arrangement!

Nora grimaced, recalling how stunned she'd felt at the betrayal. Then shocked and hurt and furious. Okay, maybe she should have confronted the two of them right then, she thought as she began removing the tiara and veil that had been intricately pinned and interwoven into her once immaculately upswept dark brown hair. But with a churchful of people waiting for the ceremony to begin, she hadn't seen the point in confrontation. Nor had she wanted to be pressured into listening to the explanations her father and Geoffrey undoubtedly had at the ready.

The bottom line was, she hadn't needed to *read* the exceedingly generous prenuptial agreement her father had given Geoff to sign to know she was about to make the biggest mistake of her life.

So...she'd done the only thing she could. She'd excused herself for "a moment alone," and written a note telling everyone—including Geoff—in no uncertain terms that the marriage was off. Then she'd grabbed her street clothes and snuck out through the rear exit of St. Paul's Cathedral and jumped into the car her father had given her as a wedding gift.

From there, it was pretty much a blur.

Nora remembered she'd been crying as she negotiated the familiar Pittsburgh streets. And with good reason. And that it had been incredibly hard to drive in a dress with such a voluminous skirt and train, even when she hiked it up over her knees and spread the beautiful lace-edged material all the way across the front seat of her brand-new Volvo station wagon.

Yet eventually she had composed herself enough to know she was not going to return to her father's home, or any other place he and Geoff would think to look for her, for quite some time—if ever! Figuring as long as she was running away, it would be nice to be somewhere warm, too, she had turned onto I-79, southbound. And despite the odd looks she kept getting from other motorists—after all, how often did anyone see a bride in her wedding dress driving *herself* anywhere, never mind one in a Volvo station wagon who was still wearing her tiara and veil?—

she'd just kept right on going. Out of Pittsburgh. Past the Pennsylvania state line, into West Virginia. Only when it began to snow and she was a good hour or so into the state had she realized she was going to have to stop and change into some warmer clothes, and probably look for someplace to wait out the storm.

But first, Nora thought, removing the last of the pins—and finally the tiara and veil—from her hair, she wanted to get a little farther south.

And, Nora thought, as she swiftly brushed out her shoulder-length hair, she wanted to get out of this dress, and away from all the reminders of how she had *almost* wrecked her life.

Dropping her brush and makeup bag in her purse, Nora snatched up the bundle of clothes she had hoped to change into and dashed out into the lobby of the tourist information center, looking for a woman who might aid her with the jammed zipper. Unfortunately, the weather being what it was, and with motorists driving like mad to get to their destinations before the snow, which was just now starting to accumulate, the building was deserted. Or at least it had been, Nora thought, taken aback as she stared in mute dismay at the only other person in the lobby.

It would have to be a lawman, she thought with a half disparaging, half wistful sigh. And a breathtakingly handsome one, at that...

SAM WHITTAKER had figured he'd run into a lot of wild and crazy things in the blizzard ahead, but a bride in a wedding dress at an interstate highway tourist information station was not one of them. Never mind one so breathtakingly beautiful she could have stepped off the cover of *Brides* magazine.

The glossy bittersweet-chocolate hue of her dark brown hair was in compelling contrast to the naturally golden hue of her skin; the mane framed her heart-shaped face and fell softly to her shoulders, like a mantle of unruly silken curls. She had a stubborn chin, a pert, turned-up nose, and softly luscious, well-shaped lips. Her dark green eyes were both spirited and innocent and flanked by a thick fringe of velvety sable lashes.

And, to Sam's consternation, her attractiveness did not end there. Tall and willowy, she was nonetheless curved in all the right places, with softly swelling breasts, a slender waist and sleekly proportioned hips.

The intricately beaded bodice of her off-the-shoulder white satin wedding gown revealed a graceful neck and elegant shoulders just right for kissing, and a collarbone that was, Sam admitted on a wave of uncensored desire, unspeakably sexy. It was a good thing she was already spoken for and he didn't believe in love at first sight, Sam thought on a wistful sigh, because if he did...he'd be tempted to whisk her away himself.

Unless... Sam stared at the woman in front of him.

No. It couldn't be, he reassured himself firmly. This woman couldn't in any way be connected to his brother, Gus, could she?

Irked that he might have been having libidinous thoughts about his future sister-in-law, Sam glanced out the plate-glass windows of the deserted lobby and worked to calm his pounding heart. Though he could see other cars slowly moving on the freeway beyond, there was only one other car in the parking lot in front of the comfort station, aside from his own black-and-white sheriff's four-wheel-drive vehicle. And that was a Volvo station wagon, which could not possibly have been Gus's, since Gus would never be caught dead in such a practical car. Gus much preferred his Lamborghini. Plus, Gus was from New York City, not Pennsylvania.

Sam breathed a sigh of relief as he turned back to the bride. Maybe this woman had nothing to do with his brother after all. Deeply ingrained manners dictating his actions, he swept off his snow-dusted Stetson hat and held it against his chest. He met her eyes. Damned, if she didn't have the most beautiful eyes and the softest lips he'd ever seen.

"Ma'am."

She lifted her head and simultaneously jerked in a breath that told him she was every bit as electrifyingly aware of him as he was of her. "Hello," she murmured in a cordial, throaty whisper.

"Are you on your way to or from your wedding?" Sam inquired, with an easy grace meant to put her immediately at ease.

She slanted him a wary glance as she sat down on a wooden bench in the lobby, hiked up her skirt a foot off the floor and dutifully exchanged a pair of wet white satin high heels for a pair of sturdy dark green rubber galoshes. "Neither, actually. The wedding's been called off," she said in a low tone.

"On account of the weather," Sam guessed, his

heart pounding at the brief glimpse of her spectacular stocking-clad legs.

She hesitated, for a moment seeming almost relieved, but said only, "It's complicated." She nodded at the bulletin board next to the floor-to-ceiling map of West Virginia that had been provided by the state to help tourists find their way. "What was that notice you were posting just now?" she asked.

Sam noted that she suddenly looked a little nervous—as she should be, given the weather. Especially if she was, as he was beginning to sense, running away from something. Like maybe the groom she'd been *supposed* to marry today...?

"It's a travelers' advisory, from the National Weather Service," Sam told her, stepping a little closer. "We're closing down the interstate, and asking everyone to take shelter as soon as possible." He'd already been advised to be on the lookout for a schoolteacher and seven schoolchildren, last seen near the Virginia-West Virginia border. And there were reports of a young mother and a baby from Maryland being tracked down, too.

The bride bit her lower lip and cast a wary look at the dark gray sky. "It's going to be that bad?"

Sam nodded gravely. "It already is, in the mountains one hundred miles south of here, next to the North Carolina border."

"When's the storm likely to hit here?" she asked, her green eyes darkened with concern. "Full force, I mean."

Sam glanced back at the snow, which was coming down in steady but moderate fashion. "It'll increase gradually during the next few hours, with maybe three to four inches on the ground at sunset. The forecasters expect it to snow steadily throughout the night. By morning, we should be really socked in.''

Her slender shoulders sagged at the news.

Figuring this was not the first bit of bad news she'd had today, Sam felt his heart go out to her, and he hastened to reassure her. ''The next exit is about five miles up the interstate from here. There are four hotels, two gas stations and several fast-food restaurants there. Last I heard, a few minutes ago, they still had rooms available. It's not a bad place to seek shelter, and I'm sure you'll be quite comfortable.''

''And it's right off the interstate?'' she asked in consternation.

''Yes,'' Sam retorted helpfully, though why that should bother her, he didn't know.

She bit her lip and gathered her skirts in her hand in order to rise. ''I see.''

For some reason Sam could not understand, the convenient location did not seem to please her. He stepped a little closer and offered her a hand. ''Listen, I hate to rush you, but given the increasing slipperiness of the roads, you and your groom should really be on your way,'' Sam said.

''I don't have a groom with me,'' she announced, with equal parts truculence and relief, as she slid her slender hand in his.

''You're here alone?'' Sam asked, stunned, as she rose gracefully to her feet.

''Completely,'' she admitted, with a beleaguered

sigh and no small amount of chagrin, as she removed her hand from his.

As the two of them stood facing each other, it was all Sam could do not to shake his head. If she was his woman, she wouldn't be running around alone—in her wedding dress—in this weather! If she was his woman, he'd see she was protected, no matter what. Especially on what was supposed to have been her wedding day. And the same went for his sister, or daughter... Where the heck were this woman's family and friends? Her maid of honor?

Her eyes lifted to his. She seemed to intuit what he was thinking but not to want to dwell on it. "Look, for obvious reasons, I really need to get out of this dress," she told him, fixing him in her sights with a pretty smile and an airy wave of her ringless left hand. "Normally, I wouldn't ask a complete stranger for assistance, but since I'm here by myself and the weather is not really conducive to satin and you are an officer of the law..."

Sam paused as his eyes locked with hers, his heart pounding against his ribs. "You want me to give you a hand?" he asked, a little hesitantly.

"Just with the zipper," she confirmed, her cheeks flushing self-consciously. "I can't see it, but it seems to be stuck." Her satin skirts rustling provocatively, she turned around in a drift of perfume, impatiently offering him her slender back. "If you could just get it started for me," she urged him anxiously, "I'm sure I can handle the rest."

"No problem," Sam murmured. Despite the easy disclaimer, his throat was as dry as the Sahara as he stepped forward to assist her. This was harder than she could imagine, but not for the reasons she'd think, Sam thought as he tried, ever so gently, to work the twisted bit of satin out of the teeth of the zipper without ripping the fine fabric. Normally, he could unkink a jammed zipper in record time. Suddenly, he was all thumbs, as he tried once again to get a better grip and wound up, instead, coming in brief, mesmerizing contact with her silky skin. And she seemed to be trembling, whether from the cold or from the inadvertent brush of his hands against her skin, he couldn't tell.

She moved from foot to foot impatiently, her breasts rising and falling beneath the beaded décolletage of her dress. Sam grimaced and forced himself to concentrate on his task, aware that his hands were tingling like crazy where they'd come in contact with her. And that she was wearing the most incredible perfume—delicate, light, floral. Like a bouquet of West Virginia wildflowers, on the first brisk day of spring...

"Can you get it?" she asked impatiently after a moment, in a low, quivering voice that did even more to his ravaged senses.

"No," Sam replied gruffly, making a low, frustrated sound in the back of his throat as he struggled with both his rising awareness of her and his blithely assigned task. "Not like this, not without ripping your dress." He dropped his hands regretfully and stepped back, aware that his pulse was pounding. And that his thoughts were not nearly as chaste or as gallant as they should be under the circumstances.

"Sorry," he growled. He paused and slanted her a

sympathetic look, able to imagine how aggravating it would be to be stuck in a wedding gown in a snowstorm. "Maybe when you get to a hotel..." he offered.

Their eyes met, and the color in her delicately sculpted cheeks deepened from a pale pink to a delicate rose. "Right." She swallowed hard. "Of course. I'll find someone—a woman—to help me there. Thanks just the same," she said hurriedly. Frowning, she reached for the bundle of clothes on the bench, then stopped and, almost as an afterthought, paused to tug a pale gray bulky-knit fisherman's sweater over her head.

Looking infinitely warmer, if a bit hilarious, with the full skirt of her wedding dress and long flowing train hanging from beneath the hem of her casual sweater, she gathered her belongings in one hand and swept up her skirt and train in the other.

Sam moved to hold the doors open for her as she swept regally toward the exit in another whisper-soft swish of satin, yards of fabric crumpled in one hand so that they wouldn't drag along the snow covering the ground.

And suddenly Sam knew he couldn't let it end there. "Let me help you to your car." Aware that he hadn't felt this gallant in a long time, Sam waited for her to pass, then strode with her out into the snow.

"Thanks, but it really isn't necessary." She tossed the words back over her shoulder, stomping determinedly past his black-and-white truck to her Volvo station wagon.

Sam saw that she was already shivering in the cold.

"I insist," he said. He followed her to the driver's-side door of the car and waited for her to press the electronic door unlock button on her key chain. When it clicked, he stepped forward to open the car door for her.

"Thanks," she murmured, bristling somewhat cantankerously, still looking as if she would much rather have done it all herself.

"You're welcome," Sam replied.

Still a little mesmerized, he watched as she tossed her bundle of belongings into the back seat, then, hitching her skirts even higher, climbed in the driver's seat. It took some doing, but finally she had pulled the gown above her knees and scrunched the fabric down enough to enable her to drive.

Sam tipped back the brim of his hat and regarded her cautiously. Though she had to be warmer with the sweater on, she couldn't possibly be comfortable behind the wheel in that dress, no matter how she squished it down or spread it out. "You sure you're going to be okay?" he asked, more sure than ever now that she was a runaway of some sort.

"I'll be just fine, Officer. Thanks for the assistance." The bride sent him a brisk, efficient smile that Sam decided was more dutiful than sincere, then shut her car door, put her key in the ignition and turned it, revving the engine.

Sam stepped back onto the curb as the motor rumbled to life with a powerful purr and the wipers moved steadily across the windshield. Out of habit, his glance lowered to the tags on the car.

A sticker on the trunk said the car had been purchased at a dealership in Pittsburgh, Pennsylvania. The vanity license plate read NO1-DATR. Sam swiftly sounded it out and decided it was meant to read Number One Daughter. He wondered whether she had chosen the slogan herself or it was a gift from a parent or parents who found it impossible to let go.

Somehow, he found himself betting it was the latter. He felt a little sorry for the parents. Because, in his estimation, this was one runaway bride who was just aching to bust free. And maybe, he thought with a grin, recalling her statement about the wedding being called off, she already had broken out and started her run for freedom.

NORA HAD NEVER BEEN ONE to swoon over a man in a uniform, but there was no denying that the handsome stranger in the snow-dusted Stetson, starched khaki uniform and thick shearling coat had made an impression on her she wasn't likely to forget. From the moment she laid eyes on his ruggedly handsome face, with its unutterably masculine features, she'd felt a peculiar electricity zigzagging through her. And that giddy awareness had only intensified when he blasted her with his boy-next-door smile.

She guessed him to be a couple years older than her own twenty-nine years. Like herself, she mused as she guided her car onto the freeway, he seemed to have a mind of his own. Plus, an easygoing nature, and the most compelling and understanding golden brown eyes she'd ever seen.

His chestnut-colored hair had been clean and soft

and cut in short layers. It had also been rumpled by either his hands or the wind and creased by his hat.

His sturdy six-foot-three-inch—if her guess was right—frame had looked athletically fit, his shoulders broad enough for a woman to lean on, more than strong enough to serve and protect.

It was too bad he was a lawman, Nora thought. Had she spent any more time with him, he'd have been bound to ask her questions she did not want to answer.

Unfortunately, right now she had worse things to worry about as she upped the speed on her windshield wipers another notch. Like how and where she was going to weather the brunt of this storm.

All she had with her, she realized, as she spotted a tow-truck driver helping a motorist whose car had slid off the road, was a suitcase full of clothes meant for a ski vacation in Vermont in the trunk, her wedding gown, and the sweater, jeans and shirt she'd worn to the salon that morning to get her hair done. Somewhere along the way, she'd lost her scarf and gloves—maybe back at the church—but she figured those could be easily replaced.

Thank goodness she had the traveler's checks and cash she'd brought along for her honeymoon, Nora thought with relief, slowing down when she saw the Road Closed Ahead signs that prevented her from going any farther on the interstate. She didn't want to use her credit cards; it would be too easy for her father to track her that way.

What she needed was to find a safe place to stay before the already slick roads became impassable.

With that in mind, Nora headed down the exit ramp
at a sedate speed. Knowing it would not be wise to
stay somewhere directly off the interstate freeway, as
those were the very first places her father would look
for her, Nora bypassed two medium-size inns, four
fast-food restaurants and a gas station, all congregated
together, and headed for the major intersection up
ahead. Once there, she paused at the directional signs
marking the two-lane county road.

Clover Creek 30.

Pleasantville 15.

Nora had never vacationed in West Virginia and
knew nothing about either town. Although, for some
odd reason, the name Clover Creek *did* seem vaguely
familiar. She searched her mind for what she knew,
but could only recall *someone*—to her frustration, she
had no idea who—once saying something about it at
a party.

*Look, it's a nice place to visit, a very nice place,
but as far as I'm concerned, being in Clover Creek
is like being at the ends of the earth....*

Wasn't that what she wanted? Nora thought as a
huge orange snowplow rumbled past her, in the direction of Clover Creek. A nice place so far off the
beaten path that no one would think to look for her
there?

Her decision made, Nora turned left and fell in behind the snowplow. She was now traveling west, not
south, but she figured it was probably the best she
could do under the circumstances. The main thing
was to find a place to bed down, where no one would
think to look for her, until the storm passed.

And since Clover Creek was only thirty miles away, the snow coming down still allowed a fair amount of visibility and the snow tires on her station wagon were gripping the pavement well, she figured she could make it, particularly with the snowplow directly in front of her, clearing the way.

TO NORA'S DELIGHT, Clover Creek was a perfect blend of old and new. A couple of inches of snow covered immaculately kept-up red brick buildings with white trim and glossy multicolored doors. From what she could tell, all the businesses were located on Main Street. On one side were a grocery store, art gallery, fabric shop, pharmacy, unisex beauty salon, hardware store, two restaurants, movie theater, newspaper and video store. On the other were a gas station, library, post office, clinic, antique shop, department store, law offices, real estate broker and police and fire stations. On streets perpendicular to Main were schools and churches. Beyond that, a number of sprawling Victorian homes on tree-lined streets.

With an inch or two of snow already on the ground, Nora had half expected the main drag in town to be deserted.

Instead, it was bustling with activity, with vehicles crowding the streets and overflowing the behind-the-building parking lots. People of all ages hurried out of the grocer's, their faces red with excitement and their arms full of bags. Others hurried out of the hardware store carrying sacks of rock salt, snow shovels, camping lanterns and chains. Still others appeared to be stocking up on books and videos. Nora did not see a hotel anywhere, but she figured a small town this busy probably had a bed-and-breakfast somewhere. Nora figured she'd get directions on where to go just as soon as she purchased a scarf and mittens for herself and found someone to help free her from her wedding dress!

As she'd expected, her presence in the gown, sweater and galoshes caused a stir. No sooner had Nora swept into the homey, shopper-laden chic of Whittakers Clothing and Department Store than she was immediately approached by three salespeople. A pretty sixty-something woman with a petite, matronly figure and a halo of fluffy pale gold curls. An equally pretty and vivacious-looking teenage girl with long golden-brown hair that fell nearly to her waist. And an older gentleman with neat salt-and-pepper hair and a matching, well-trimmed beard.

Wasting no time, the woman greeted Nora with a warm smile and a twinkle in her eyes. "I'm Clara Whittaker." She extended a hand, then made introductions briefly. "This is my husband, Harold, and my granddaughter Kimberlee."

"Hello. It's nice to meet you all. You can call me Nora." She'd prefer not to use last names, but clearly, Nora thought, they were so friendly and so informal, *something* in the way of a greeting was required.

"That's a lovely wedding dress...." Kimberlee said.

"Thanks." Nora smiled at the teen as she selected a warm green-and-black wool scarf and matching insulated mittens and carried them to the counter.

"Getting married soon?" Clara Whittaker asked, smiling all the more.

"I was hoping to...." Nora said honestly. *Someday, when I met my Mr. Right.*

Smiling broadly, Clara Whittaker looked behind Nora. While her husband began ringing up Nora's purchase, Clara smoothed a hand down the folds of her neat corduroy shirtdress. Her light brown eyes twinkling merrily, she said, "I don't see your groom."

Nora gave them all an it's-a-long-story, one-I'm-really-not-at-liberty-to-reveal look. "My...er...um... groom is not here with me right now," she said finally, after a great deal of wrestling with her conscience.

"Do you know when he'll be here?" Kimberlee asked inquisitively, taking the sensors off Nora's purchases.

"No, I don't know when—" *or even if,* Nora amended silently "—he'll catch up with me. Probably not before the storm descends upon us full blast, though."

Deciding to change the subject before any more questions were asked of her that required honest—if uncomfortable—replies, Nora turned to the framed poster of Gus Whittaker and two of the New York Knicks displayed on the wall. "Are you related to the Gus Whittaker?"

Clara and Harold nodded proudly as Harold bagged Nora's purchases. "He's our grandson."

"Really," Nora said. So Gus Whittaker was the one who'd been talking about Clover Creek. *That* was why she remembered it. Why was everyone grinning as though they knew a secret or something? she wondered.

Nora searched through her billfold and extricated enough cash to pay for her purchases. "I met him several years ago, when I was working for Leland and Brooks, an advertising agency in New York City. Several of Gus's clients were—are—celebrity spokespersons for L and B's key accounts. Hence, Gus and his celebrity clients were invited to all the L and B parties. And, well, you know Gus." Nora smiled and gestured inanely. "He makes it a point to seek out all the young, available females."

"Did the two of you hit it off, right from the first moment you met?" Kimberlee asked, stars in her eyes.

Nora flushed; she didn't know quite how to answer that. Clearly, Gus's whole family adored him, and they seemed to have already decided that was what had happened. "Well, yes," Nora replied carefully after a moment. Then she hastened to add, "Although that first meeting was pretty hectic, with all the people at the party, the noise and the confusion…"

"Of course…" Everyone nodded.

A bell sounded, signaling that someone else had come into the store. Nora turned, her jaw dropping open slightly as she saw the sexy sheriff she'd met earlier stride toward the group. She stared at the lawman as he walked across the polished wood floor, hardly able to believe they'd crossed paths again!

"But later you got to know Gus better…?" Clara asked.

Nora had temporarily lost her hearing, her sense of sight draining all her other faculties.

Her heart pounding, she turned away from the sexy sheriff, who was heading her way. "Um, yes, I guess you could say that." Nora smiled at Gus's family, wanting to say something pleasant about the Whittakers' grandson. "Everyone in the sports management business tries to emulate Gus these days—he's that successful." If unconventional in the extreme... "And a very nice guy, as well."

Again, everyone beamed proudly at the compliments Nora bestowed on Gus.

A quick glance revealed that the sheriff was talking to other shoppers in the store, but he still had Nora in his sights. Whether he was on to the particulars of her plight or not, Nora could not tell.

"So, when's Gus arriving in Clover Creek?" Harold asked as the sheriff eventually came to a halt beside Nora and the others.

Nora blinked, as thrown by the abrupt switch in topics as she was by the lawman's deliberate pursuit of, and proximity to, her. "I really couldn't say," she replied, somewhat hoarsely, not sure why they were asking *her* that. "I haven't talked to Gus lately."

"But you will soon?" Clara pressed. As the lawman stepped even closer to her, Nora was inundated by the clean, woodsy scent of his cologne.

"I—don't know," Nora hedged slowly, not wanting to hurt or offend any of Gus's family.

Harold smiled, looked at the sheriff, and then back at Nora. "Have you met Sam yet?"

Nora blinked. "Who?"

Harold winked at Nora slyly, even as he gestured at the sheriff warmly. "Our other grandson!"

Nora took a calming breath as she and the sheriff stared at each other in contemplative silence. Oh, no—no! "You're—?"

"Gus Whittaker's younger brother, Sam," he confirmed with a tantalizing grin as he swaggered closer and his gaze moved across her upturned face. "And you're...?"

Suffused with heat everywhere his eyes had roved, Nora swallowed and stepped back. "Nora," she said simply, deciding to leave it at that. Dear heaven, this was a complication she did not need. Especially now!

"Nora," Sam repeated, as if liking the sound of her name. He studied her, then asked, in a soft, low voice laced with laughter, "Do you have a last name?"

"Yes," Nora replied, as she looked into his golden-brown eyes with all the directness she could muster. "It's..."

"She's one of Gus's very good, shall we say, *friends*, from New York City," Harold supplied helpfully.

"Wait," Nora corrected hastily, holding up a palm in traffic-cop fashion. "I never said Gus and I were actually, you know, buddies—" She and Gus were more like acquaintances. Remote acquaintances.

"We know you didn't, dear," Clara patted her arm forgivingly.

"We know Gus would want to tell us himself," Harold beamed.

"Tell you what?" Nora wheezed, perplexed.

"About his plans, of course," Clara said.

Nora regarded the Whittakers cautiously. She felt as if she'd landed in a TV sitcom. One of the wacky, humor-filled kinds that didn't necessarily have to make a lot of sense. "What are you talking about?" she demanded warily, already dreading the reply.

"Sweetheart, it's all right, *we know*," Harold counseled her warmly.

Sensing that whatever they were talking about, they were deadly serious, Nora fought to contain her mounting exasperation. "Know what?" she cried, upset.

Clara beamed, her own happiness evident. "You're Gus's fiancée!"

Chapter Two

Nora took a deep breath and tried, as nicely as possible, to explain. "I know there's been a lot of confusion today, what with the storm and all, but Gus and I are *not* getting married, today or any other day."

All around her, faces fell in obvious disappointment.

"Then why are you in that dress?" Kimberlee Whittaker asked, perplexed, as she propped her hands on her waist. "And why did you come to Clover Creek at precisely 3:30 this afternoon?"

Good question, Nora thought. She could just as easily have gone the other way back at the crossroads. What had brought her here to Clover Creek? she wondered. Destiny?

Sam's eyes held hers. "I'd like to hear the answer to that myself," he drawled.

Nora knew she was not going to get anyone to help her unjam the zipper and get out of the dress until she explained. "I'm afraid there's been some misunderstanding," Nora said, looking straight at Sam. Who seemed, oddly enough, to be the only one not harboring a hope that she would change course and *marry* Gus. She paused to draw a bracing breath. "I don't know where everyone got the idea I'm in love with your brother," she began, uncomfortably embarrassed, "but I assure you, nothing could be further from the truth! Gus and I are..." Nora groped for a way to explain. "Well, *friends,* sort of, and that's all!"

At that, everyone regarded her so skeptically that it was all Nora could do not to groan out loud. "No one believes me, do they?" she asked Sam as a curious group of customers gathered round.

"Wouldn't appear so, no." Sam paused, his glance sliding over her approvingly before returning to focus on the self-conscious flush in her cheeks. "But there's a simple way to clear this up. Just explain who you are, where you're from and who you were really planning to marry today."

Nora was tired of men telling her what to do! She crossed her arms in front of her and stubbornly dug in her heels. "I don't see why I have to explain anything," she retorted mutinously. Hadn't she already revealed enough of her private life?

Sam shrugged. "Then don't."

"Fine." Nora shrugged right back at him. Deciding she'd looked into the depths of his eyes long enough, she turned her glance away. "I won't."

"But if you want to calm all the questions about you and Gus and what might or might not be going on," Sam continued, "you will."

And have someone then take it upon himself to decide to play hero and call her father? As much as the dutiful-daughter part of her wanted to allay her father's worries, the part of her that had had enough knew she could not deal with her dad, not yet. Forgetting for a moment all the others gathered around them, Nora regarded Sam sternly. "Look, I already told you my wedding was called off," she said, making no effort to hide her exasperation with him.

"When did this happen?" Clara asked, as even more customers gathered round to hear.

"At the tourist station on the freeway, an hour ago," Nora replied in an aside.

"You two met?" Harold gasped.

"Briefly," Sam acknowledged reluctantly, his glance still heating her like a fierce blanket.

"And what little I said to you then is really all I intend to say on the matter," Nora continued firmly. Like it or not, Sam and the Whittakers and everyone else in Clover Creek were all just going to have to accept that.

Fortunately for her, just then the phone began to ring.

Her stunned gaze still on Nora, Clara picked up the receiver. "Whittakers Department Store," Clara said, then broke into a broad grin. "Gus, darling! We've all been waiting to hear from you! Hang on a minute, dear, while I put you on the speakerphone," Clara said. She punched a few buttons and paused to confirm that he was still there before continuing, "Now, where are you, sweetheart?"

"Stuck in the city!" Gus Whittaker shouted from the other end. In the background, a horn blared and brakes squealed. The moment the background noise subsided, Gus lowered his voice and asked, somewhat anxiously, "Listen, Gran, did the pretty lady arrive okay?"

Everyone turned to Nora and grinned, as if her "secret" had been revealed.

She couldn't help it; she blushed.

"I'm happy to report the pretty lady is here, and all in one piece!" Clara replied cheerfully. "But I must say we'd all be a little happier if you had only been here to witness her arrival, too!"

"I know, but—" Gus uttered a wistful sigh, then chuckled. "Isn't she a beaut?"

"And then some," Sam replied, with no hint of irony, as he turned back to Nora.

Her pulse automatically increased.

"You'll take good care of her until I can arrive?" Gus continued to worry on the other end. "Find someplace safe and warm and dry for her to stay? Maybe over at your house, Gran?"

"Don't you worry, Gus. We'll make room for her," Sam said.

"Great." On the other end, Gus breathed an audible sigh of relief. "When I get there, we'll see about changing her name."

At that, winks and nods were exchanged all around. Sam regarded her intently. Nora, helpless to prevent what they were all concluding, could only roll her eyes.

More horns sounded in the background, on the other end of the line. "Well, listen, I better go—" Gus said.

Clara frowned. "Wait. Don't you want to talk to

anyone else?'' she asked her grandson quickly. *Meaning me, of course,* Nora thought.

"Gee, I'd love to, Gran," Gus replied, "but..." A horn blared, obliterating his voice. Gus swore as the sounds of sirens increased in the background. "There's an..." Static crackled. "...ambulance..." Brakes squealed. "trying to..." Another horn blared. "...get through...." The siren rose to an earsplitting shriek before it faded slightly. "....later," Gus said in a muffled tone.

The click of the connection being severed was followed by utter silence, as once again all eyes turned Nora's way.

"I really don't know what to say," she said, blushing. She knew what they were thinking. She could hardly blame them. It had sounded as if Gus were talking about a woman arriving, as a surprise to his family, and since she was the only newcomer around, for the moment, anyway, they were assuming—quite wrongly, as it happened—that it was her.

"That's all right, dear, you don't have to say another word," Clara Whittaker said, patting Nora's hand gently. "I think we've all figured out what's going on."

Everyone looked at each other. After a moment, they all began to grin and talk at once. "It really is obvious," someone put in finally.

A farmer in overalls and a bill cap chuckled merrily. "The pretty lady here and Gus had a fight—"

"He was probably late getting out of the city—like he said on the phone just now," added a woman in a parka and jeans.

"And then, naturally, their plans got all messed up—" a teen Kimberlee's age said.

"Who wouldn't be ticked off?" a white-haired woman put in indignantly. "Gus should have put her—and their impending nuptials—first on their wedding day."

"Typical Gus, though," said a nicely dressed young woman with a toddler in tow. "Business first, then pleasure."

Another woman, in an upscale running suit and sneakers, chuckled. "'Course, he makes up for it when he does party. There's no one who can throw a bash like Gus!"

Nora threw up her hands in frustration and broke into the conversation. "For the last time, everyone! I am not engaged to Gus Whittaker!"

"Not anymore," a handsome young man in construction clothes said, grinning and nodding at the bare ring finger on Nora's left hand.

"Don't worry, honey, when he shows up and proposes all over again, I'm sure he'll bring you your ring," an older man added.

"Unless..." Clara paused, a worried look on her face. "You didn't throw it away in a fit of pique, did you?"

"No, I didn't throw it away!" Nora exclaimed stiffly as she tightened her grip on her package and started to brush by Sam. "Because I never had a ring from him in the first place."

Kimberlee Whittaker gasped as Sam stepped back slightly to allow Nora to pass.

"All the more reason to delay the nuptials, then," Kimberlee said indignantly.

"Really," another woman added fervently, in support. "Gus should get you a ring, and we—his friends and neighbors—will make sure he does."

Nora groaned, and shot a glance at Sam, who was still regarding her with an interest that had little, if anything, to do with local law enforcement. With an effort, she tore her eyes from his and turned back to the crowd gathered round her. "Trust me. If Gus shows up before I leave Clover Creek, and that in itself is doubtful, given the fact Gus's still in New York City as we speak, Gus is *not* going to ask me to marry him. Not in a million years," she promised them all firmly.

Sam Whittaker continued to contemplate her—and her current predicament. "The breakup was that harsh?" Sam asked, in a low, sexy voice that sent shivers down Nora's spine.

"There was no breakup," Nora said, looking straight at Sam, before finishing in utter exasperation, "We were never together."

SAM KNEW no one else in the store did, but he believed Nora, for a variety of reasons. He also thought, from the guilty way she was flushing and the slightly nervous way she was behaving, that she was hiding a lot more than she was telling, and that she might need help. His help. In any case, it was almost certain that there were a lot of people worried about her.

Unlike Nora, however, he did not believe in running from problems; he knew predicaments were best dealt with directly. He hoped, before she left Clover Creek, to convince her of that, too. And perhaps reunite her with her friends and family, as well.

"Then who were you engaged to?" Sam asked Nora, aware that he really wanted to know not just that, but everything about her. Furthermore, he hoped she'd tell him more about herself, now that she'd seen firsthand how insatiably curious the small, friendly West Virginia community could be.

"I'd rather not say, Sam."

"How about your last name, then?"

She glared at him for a moment. "I don't see what that matters—"

"It does if you're going to be staying here. Unless there's a reason you don't want any of us to know who you really are." He was baiting her, anxious to see her reaction to that.

Nora's mouth opened in a round O of surprise then snapped shut. She paused, looking as reluctant as any runaway would, but in the end, as he'd figured she would, came through.

"It's Hart-Kingsley. Nora Hart-Kingsley. My mother's name was Hart, my father's Kingsley. I ended up with both family names. Satisfied?"

Sam grinned. "It's a start," he said. Although he would need a lot more than that, if he was going to be able to help her.

Dr. Ellen Maxwell stepped between Sam and Nora, swiftly introducing herself as the town physician before saying, "If you want me to put my two cents in, I think it's just as well the nuptials get delayed a while, anyway. The weather would not make it easy for any out-of-town guests—never mind the groom—to get here.''

''And besides, if you're going to be a part of the Whittaker clan, you need time to get to know the rest of us, too,'' Kimberlee said.

Nora regarded the people gathered around her. ''Isn't anyone going to listen to me?'' she demanded, in obvious exasperation. Though they obviously meant well.

The group replied in unison. ''No.''

Harold patted Nora's shoulder in a comforting manner. ''It's okay, honey. We all know how to act stunned and amazed. We can do that for Gus. We won't ruin his surprise for us.''

Clara smiled. ''In the meantime, maybe you'd like to get out of that dress, and see about doing something to dry the hem and train—it looks a little damp, from where I'm standing.''

Good idea, Nora thought, if only because it'd stop all the wedding talk.

''The only problem is, there's something wrong with the zipper,'' Nora confided. ''We may have to cut me out of it. So if I could borrow some scissors and enlist a little help, after I dash out to my car to get a change of clothes, I'll—''

Clara patted her arm. ''Now, now, I'm sure we can fix it without making any cuts in this beautiful fabric. Kim, darling, help Nora get her clothes out of her car and then show Nora to a dressing room and help her out of that gown.''

''Right, Gran,'' Kimberlee said, giving a thumbs-up sign before leading the way.

"YOU'RE just going to have to ignore Sam," Kimberlee told Nora as she worked on the jammed zipper in the back of Nora's dress.

Nora turned, the trailing satin hem of her wedding gown swishing softly across the parquet floor of the large, old-fashioned fitting room. "What do you mean?"

Kimberlee tossed the length of her golden-brown hair off her shoulders. She paused and took a tiny drop of liquid soap and ever so delicately worked it into the teeth of the zipper. "I saw those looks he was giving you," Kimberlee said, catching Nora's glance in the three-way mirror before peering down at the zipper seam. "The way he questioned you."

Nora flushed. "I think he's just curious."

Kimberlee shook her head. In an electric-purple jumper and ribbed white turtleneck, purple tights and cute leather ankle boots, she looked pretty enough to be on the cover of a teen magazine. "It's more than that. He thinks it's his job to take care of everyone!"

Alarm bells went off in Nora's head. Perspiration broke her skin. "Because he's the sheriff?" Nora asked warily—aware that she was flushing again, an even brighter pink.

"Because he's Sam."

"You're saying he's controlling?" Nora asked, as casually as possible.

"To the max," Kimberlee affirmed emotionally. "It's because of Mom and Dad and the way they—" At the sound of footsteps in the hallway outside the fitting room, Kimberlee stopped short and stuck her head out into the hall to see who was there. Almost immediately, she flushed a bright red. "Sam!"

Sam looked at his younger sister grimly as he stepped inside the spacious fitting room. Obviously, Nora thought, Sam did not appreciate whatever it was his younger sister had been about to reveal. Which was too bad, because Nora found herself wanting to know everything there was to know about Sam that Sam didn't want revealed.

"You're needed out front to help ring up the purchases," Sam told Kimberlee firmly.

Kimberlee gave her older brother a pouty look. "Can't you help out? After all, you used to work in the store, too, when you were my age. You know how to do it."

Sam leaned against the door frame, clearly in no hurry to go anywhere. "I'm not disputing that, but Gran wants you."

"Ha!" Kimberlee said. "I think you just want to be back here with Nora." Kimberlee gave Nora a commiserating look as she flounced out. "Good luck. You're going to need it with Mr. Impossible here!"

"Mr. Impossible?" Nora echoed when Kimberlee had left.

"It's one of the nicer things she's called me lately," Sam said dryly as Nora surreptitiously measured the dwindling distance between them as he advanced all the way into the room.

He had dispensed with the Stetson and shearling coat and brushed the snow from his pants and shoes. And though Nora should've expected that—if Sam Whittaker were spending any time at all inside the heated building—she hadn't expected the way he would look in the snug-fitting khaki uniform. He had an all-business stance that suggested he didn't take trouble from anyone, but it was more than just that, and the come-hither look in his eyes, that had her pulse racing. It was his commanding height, the dwarfing width of his shoulders. The muscular tightness of his lean hips and long legs. And, most of all, the way he was looking at her now that made her tingle from head to toe.

"Still stuck, hmm?" he drawled, looking over at her almost insolently.

In this town, in her dress, in her whole life, Nora thought. "Maybe we should just give up and cut me out of this dress," Nora suggested.

Sam continued to look her up and down as Nora grew ever warmer. "Oh, I think we can do better than that," he quipped. "Wait here. I'll be right back."

Nora barely had time to draw a brush through the wind-mussed layers of her dark hair before he returned with a buttonhook and a pair of tweezers.

"Don't look so worried," Sam said cheerfully as he stepped behind Nora. His eyes met and held hers in the mirror. "I'm an experienced hand at this. I'm sure I can free you from this dress."

Something about the utterly male way he was looking at her made Nora sure he could, too. And that might be even more dangerous. "You didn't have much luck earlier, back at the tourist station," she said breathlessly as he placed his hands lightly on her shoulders.

"Ah, but I didn't have the right tools then," he told her. "Now I do."

Nora raised a skeptical brow as the back of his hand brushed the bare skin at the nape of her neck. She froze beneath the onslaught of his touch, the warmth and gentleness of his skin pressed against hers. He had just come close to her, and she was ablaze already. She could barely breathe.

Aware that her heart was beating wildly in her chest, she forced herself to concentrate not on what they shouldn't be doing—ever—but on what he was actually doing now. Aloud, she asked, "A buttonhook and tweezers are the right tools for an occasion such as this?"

Sam's gaze met hers, and his handsome golden-brown eyes lit enthusiastically. "You'd be surprised what can be accomplished with these two items, under the right circumstances," he said with mock graveness, as he bent his head and once again concentrated on his task.

Nora hitched in a breath, realizing that, friend or foe, it didn't seem to matter. With every second that passed, she became even more extraordinarily aware of him.

"You don't have to do this, you know," she told him defiantly, as she noticed that her knees were trembling, and that the shiver ghosting down her spine had nothing to do with the cold weather outside and everything to do with the heat generated by Sam.

"Actually," Sam drawled, as he ever-so-carefully grasped the jammed fabric with the tweezers and slid the end of the buttonhook between the fabric and the teeth of the zipper to gently move them in tandem. "I do."

Nora's brow lifted as he continued to labor over the back of her dress with delicate finesse. *What did he know that she didn't?*

"I came in here on a mission," he explained.

Nora waited until he'd finished whatever it was he was doing to her zipper, then spun around to confront him face-to-face. "That mission being?"

"To find out if you need help of some sort. Because if you do," Sam vowed, setting both buttonhook and tweezers aside, "I'm here to give it."

EVEN KNOWING what Nora did about the error of her ways, she was tempted to let herself be rescued. But letting a man jump in to save her from all life's hardships was what had gotten her into this mess in the first place. It was high time she stood on her own two feet and said adios to *all* well-meaning, overbearing men. Her chin took on a challenging tilt. "And if I don't need help?" she asserted calmly, her heart pounding.

Sam shrugged. "Then you don't," he retorted mildly, though it was clear he did not think that was the case.

Nora sighed. She could see Sam was not going to be an easy man to dissuade. No doubt he would shadow her as long as she remained in Clover Creek. "You know," she said, stepping back to lean against the far wall, her hands pressed flat behind her, "since we're alone, I have a bone to pick with you."

Sam took up a post against the opposite wall, only a few feet away. He folded his arms in front of him and kept his eyes trained on her face. "That bone being?"

Nora tilted her face up to his and drew a deep breath. "So far, this has been one of the worst days of my life. And you are *not* making things any easier on me with all your prying questions."

He nodded, accepting that. Then said, with a devilish gleam in his eyes, "It was never my intention to make it easy on you."

Her heart beating all the harder, Nora met his eyes. "Why not?"

Sam dropped his hands to his sides and continued regarding her steadily. "'Cause my gut instinct tells me it's the fact you've been way too sheltered in the past that has you running away now."

Nora struggled to hold her rising temper in check. She hated it when a man presumed to know—via ESP or, worse, *experience with other women!*—what was on her mind. "How do you know I'm running away?" she demanded.

"Isn't it obvious?" Sam straightened and pushed away from the wall. "You've been acting like you had something to hide since the first moment we met. Now, I don't know what hurt you so. And don't bother to deny it. You have been hurt. I can see it in your eyes whenever the subject of your wedding comes up. But I'd like to find out," he told her as he slowly stepped toward her.

"So I've been hurt," Nora retorted nervously, straightening as he neared. "Everyone has."

"That's true." Sam planted a hand against the wall on either side of her. "But not everyone takes off in their wedding dress in the midst of what will soon be a blizzard—''

Nora interrupted hotly, in self-defense. "I didn't know it was going to snow!"

Sam looked down at her as if he found *that* very hard to swallow. He shook his head wordlessly and leaned in even closer. "How could you not have known that?" he asked, very, very softly, the heat of his body emanating to hers.

Nora flushed and responded wryly, "Because, Mr. I-Gotta-Have-All-the-Answers, I wasn't *listening* to the weather reports this morning, or last night, for that matter!"

"Why not?" His voice was hushed, seductive, his breath warm on her skin, as he placed his hands on the bare curves of her shoulders and forced her to look up at him.

Nora ignored the sensual feeling of his palms on her bare skin. They were slightly chapped and callused, as though he knew firsthand the value of hard physical work, but tender, too, as if he knew how to love. Irritated with herself—after all, she had no business thinking like that!—Nora shook off the sensual image of her body, in his hands.

"Because I had a ton of other important things to do!" she answered, with a regal toss of her head. "I had to get up early and shower and go to the hairdresser, and then over to the church, to dress and get my official wedding portrait done." She stopped and bit her lip, aware that he was suddenly looking very much as though he wanted to do a whole lot more than simply hold her in front of him. He wanted to kiss her! Not just once, but probably again and again and again!

Sam grinned and lifted a skeptical golden-brown brow. "Are you saying the rest of your wedding party didn't know it was going to snow, either?"

"Maybe not." Nora swallowed around the sudden tightness of her throat. Looking deep into Sam's eyes, she could almost believe he wanted only to help her. "After all, the snowstorm is not supposed to hit Pi—uh..." She made a strangled sound, as she realized she'd inadvertently said far too much, and cut herself off in midsentence.

"Pittsburgh?" Sam supplied, his hands following the curve of her shoulders and caressing her bare arms.

Nora glared at him defiantly and tried to ignore the enticing scent that was him. "What makes you think the wedding was supposed to take place in Pittsburgh?"

"The license plates on your car," Sam replied, looking so abruptly earnest and helpful and forthright, it was all she could do not to melt into the warmth of his embrace.

"Also," he said frankly, "the geography fits. If the wedding was supposed to take place sometime this morning, as I am guessing it was, you had time to drive from Pittsburgh down to West Virginia. You did not have time to drive from, say, New York City to West Virginia since this morning."

She stared at him, the concern on his face unnerving her more than she wanted to admit. "You noticed the plates on my car?" she asked, feeling the color drain from her face. That meant he could trace her origins quicker than she could say "One-two-three." And from there go directly to her father and Geoff!

Sam shrugged and, dropping his hands from her shoulders, stepped back slightly. "I'm a lawman," he explained matter-of-factly. "I'm trained to notice everything."

And that seemed to go triple where she was concerned, Nora thought, her insides inexplicably heating all the more.

Nora sighed. Maybe this initial mix-up wasn't as bad as she'd thought—especially if it kept her from being traced back to her father and Geoff. She studied Sam. "You don't think I'm engaged to your brother," she stated, rather than asked.

"You know I don't," Sam replied with a seductive half grin.

"Why not?" Nora demanded, shocked to find things suddenly going her way. Or were they? "Everyone else does."

Sam shrugged his impossibly broad shoulders and kept his eyes on hers. "You're not his type," Sam said, in a very low, very definite tone of voice.

His confidence in his ability to analyze and understand her was supremely irritating, as was the way she melted at his slightest touch or look. Nora cautioned herself to keep her defenses up or suffer the consequences.

"Oh, really." Nora bristled at the sexy stranger who was fast proving to be her nemesis. "Then whose type am I?" she demanded archly.

Sam hooked an arm about her waist and pulled her into the tantalizing warmth of his embrace. "Mine."

Chapter Three

"You're not just nosy," Nora sputtered. "You're nuts!"

Sam grinned victoriously, his hot glance skimming her from head to toe. "Can I help it if I know what I want?"

"You also know I was supposed to get married today."

"And yet, when you talk about not getting married," he scoffed, using the arm anchored around her waist to bring her even closer, "you look nothing but relieved."

"So maybe my fiancé was not my Mr. Right," Nora theorized hotly.

He grinned at her display of temper, his glance taking in the bare curves of her shoulders before returning with sensual deliberation to her eyes. He stared at her with taunting intensity. "And maybe in running away the way you did, even if it was at the very last minute, you stopped yourself from making the biggest mistake of your life."

Suffused with heat everywhere Sam's eyes had gazed, as well as everywhere they had not, Nora swallowed. She wished she was wearing anything but this beaded white satin wedding dress, with its flirtatiously full skirt and long, closely fitted drop sleeves and bosom-revealing neckline.

Determined not to let Sam get the better of her, in conversation or anything else, she made herself take a tranquilizing breath.

"As it happens," Nora told Sam, glad at last that someone understood she'd prevented a mistake in running away, not made one, "that's precisely what I did."

Slowly he lowered his face to hers. His golden-brown eyes glittered rapaciously. "Then I've got nothing to worry about, even if your groom does show up here to reclaim you, do I?" he asked in a soft, silken voice.

Fighting the electric heat Sam's touch elicited, Nora relaxed slightly in the comforting cradle of his arms. "I don't think he'll come after me," Nora replied sadly. "And even if he did, it wouldn't make any difference."

"Good." Satisfaction filled his eyes as he dropped one hand from around her back and lifted her chin to his.

"Why do you say that?"

Still gazing deep into her eyes, he curved his hand around her cheek and chin. "Because I'm old enough to know that chemistry like this comes but once in a lifetime, and I want my own chance with you," he said softly.

Nora threw up her hands. She'd never met anyone more persistent. Furthermore, she knew by the confident, controlled way Sam held himself that he would never be satisfied unless he held the upper hand. And wasn't that what she was trying to get away from? Men who would rule her life?

"Don't you care that I'm on the rebound?" She pushed the words through clenched teeth, finding it hard to hang on to her cool.

Sam merely grinned from ear to ear. "Are you?" Sam asked, leaning forward. As he did so, his lips touched her temple. "'Cause I could've sworn by the way you've been acting today that you never really loved this Mr. Wrong of yours in the first place." He paused and looked deep into her eyes.

He hadn't even tried to kiss her lips, though he could have, and he was merely touching her face, yet Nora's nipples tightened painfully beneath her lacy bridal corset. Lower still, there was a definite pressure building, and a new weakness in her knees. And the startling desire to feel his lips on hers—not just in a momentary experiment, but in a passionate explosion of feeling that went on...well, indefinitely.

And that, Nora thought, was crazy. She didn't even know this man! Furthermore, she was not the kind of woman who could be swept off her feet. Not ever. And yet it appeared, she thought as she drew a shaky breath, that Sam Whittaker was doing just that.

"You didn't love him, did you?" Sam probed.

Nora's eyes widened at the low, masculine promise in his voice. "N-no," she said as color poured into the high, sculpted planes of her face.

"Good," Sam replied in a low, gravelly voice. "Then that's all I need to know," he said, pulling her

against him. He threaded one hand through her hair.
His lips grazed hers, tenderly at first, then with building passion. Nora was engulfed by so many sensations and feelings at once. The woodsy scent of him,
the minty taste of his mouth. His lips were sure and
sensual, his body was hard and warm. The man knew
how to kiss! Knew how to draw a thrilling, incredibly
sensual response from her, the kind she had read
about but never really dreamed existed. And it was
only then, when Nora realized what Sam had done to
her, in getting her to respond that way to him, that
he slowly drew back.

Not sure she could stand unassisted, Nora wreathed
her arms about his shoulders and held on tight. Her
heart slammed against her ribs, and she could barely
catch her breath as she stared up at him.

He looked down at her, breathing just as erratically,
appearing just as stunned, just as pleased. He smiled
at her then, ever so softly and reluctantly, released his
grip on her. "You're free now."

Nora blinked up at him dizzily, aware that she'd
never felt more lovestruck than she did at that moment. "To love again?" she asked.

Sam ran his fingertips down the open wedge of the
back of her gown, eliciting another series of tin-
gles—and the realization that her troublesome zipper
was no longer jammed. "To get out of the dress."

"Oh." Embarrassed at the unspeakably ardent direction of her thoughts, Nora started to step away
from the dressing room wall.

Sam planted a hand on either side of her and leaned

in close. "But don't give up on the other," he told her softly. "You're free to do that, too."

Looking deep into Sam's eyes, Nora could almost believe that it was all that simple. She wanted Sam—at least for now; she should have him. But common sense prevailed, telling her this was not the type of diversion she should be allowing herself, not when she still had so much about her life to sort out. Like where she was going to live, and how she was going to get her father to listen to her and stop meddling in her life. And she had to do all that without completely destroying the only familial relationship she had left in her life in the process.

Determined to put first things first, Nora flattened a hand across Sam's chest and pressed against the solid male warmth. But before she could speak, the pager attached to his belt began a steady, insistent beep.

The edges of Sam's mouth tightened into a frown.

As he reached down to turn off the pager, his eyes met hers. "Guess I'll see you later," he drawled.

Nora sighed. Whether it was wise or not, she had been afraid that would be the case.

WHEN NORA CAME OUT of the dressing room some fifteen minutes later, her wedding gown folded and looped over her arms, the crowd in Whittakers had barely thinned. People were still lined up in droves, purchasing gloves, hats and snow boots, chatting excitedly about the three or so inches of snow that were now on the ground.

Before Nora could do more than smile a hello at

another group of curious townspeople, her wedding dress was taken from her—for drying and pressing, Clara said—and she was introduced all around. As a "special friend" of Gus's. After which the conversation promptly returned to—what else?—the weather, and the effect it was likely to have on the town in the days to come.

"I hope this storm doesn't interfere with our silent auction for the EMS Fund," Wynnona Kendrick, the florist, said.

"We're saving up for a new ambulance," Doc Ellen explained to Nora as her five-year-old daughter, Katie, tried to decide between two pairs of insulated ski mittens. "We've been working on it for almost a year, and so far we've only raised five thousand dollars. Unless we can find a way to raise money more quickly, at the rate we're going it'll take us five more years to get one."

"What are you auctioning off?" Nora asked, wondering if there was any way she could be of help.

"Quilts, crafts, paintings, homemade jams, candies, handcrafted furniture and cookbooks. You name it, we'll probably have it over at the high school gym come Wednesday evening," Doc Ellen replied, putting the mittens Katie had selected on the counter for ringing up.

"Unless the snow still has the roads impassable," Clara Whittaker interjected, with a worried look.

"In which case, we'll simply delay it." Doc Ellen searched Nora's face. "You'll come, won't you?"

"Sure, if I'm still here," Nora promised. *If not, I'll*

make a donation. She smiled, adding, "It sounds like a worthy cause."

"It is. And it'll be fun, too, 'cause we've got the whole community involved."

Silence fell.

Afraid the talk was going to turn to her canceled wedding again, Nora asked, "Where did Sam go?" And why did she have the feeling *he* could save her from all this?

"Fender bender at the high school," Harold Whittaker replied, as he rang up a pair of long johns for a customer. "No one hurt, and only one car involved, but there's a stop sign and park bench that used to be in better shape. Why?" Sam's grandfather peered at her curiously from over the rim of his old-fashioned spectacles. "Did you need to talk to Sam?"

What Nora needed was to find out whether her father and Geoffrey had set up the alarm for her in West Virginia. If they had, it was probably through the police departments of the state. And the key to that information was Sam. "Yes, I do," she replied.

"Well, he should be back in the sheriff's office soon." Harold smiled warmly. "If you want to go over there and wait on him, I'm sure he wouldn't mind."

SAM GOT BACK to the office seconds before Nora breezed in.

"So, this is what a small-town sheriff's office looks like." Nora said breathlessly as she tugged her mittens off with her teeth, unfastened the wooden toggle buttons on her coat and took a moment to look around.

While Sam watched Nora with the same unabashed curiosity with which she was studying everything else, Nora's glance moved quickly over the two battered oak desks, set several feet apart, and several black metal file cabinets in the small square room.

She paused before a computer and printer, looked over the bulletin board covered with Wanted posters, the fax machine and copier. If she noted that the equipment was more functional than state-of-the-art, she made no comment. And, instead, turned her attention to the enormous shortwave radio and the reconditioned IBM typewriter Sam and the other deputies used to fill out forms.

Finished with her survey of the reception area and office that spanned the front of the brick building, Nora peeked out the doorway, into the hall that ran the length of the middle of the building. She turned back to Sam. "May I?"

He nodded.

There was no one else there. It wouldn't hurt for her to look around. Everyone else in town had, at one time or another.

He followed her past the rest rooms and the soda and coffee machines, to the single jail cell, with its two cots. Both were unoccupied, as was usually the case.

Nora studied the metal cots, which were outfitted with white cotton sheets and blue wool blankets, then turned back to Sam. Together, they walked out into the front office again.

"I'm surprised," Nora murmured, as she took off her green wool parka and hung it on the tree rack next to the door. "I didn't expect so much modern equipment."

Sam hadn't expected Nora to look every bit as ravishingly beautiful in a white shirt, gray pewter sweater and jeans as she had in her elegantly beaded white satin wedding dress.

"I had to fight for every piece of it."

She flashed him an appreciative smile. "You must've been pleased to get it," she said.

"I was. It's hard to do my job effectively without it."

Nora's glance moved once again to the Wanted notices on the bulletin board as Sam assumed a seat. "What sort of things do you get on the fax?" she asked.

Sam kicked back in his chair and propped his feet on the edge of his desk. "Between the insurance companies and the state and federal government, there's never any shortage of paperwork. And, of course, notices from other law enforcement agencies."

"Is your computer connected into the Internet?" Nora asked.

Sam nodded, his mind drifting back to the kiss they'd shared in the dressing room over at Whittakers. He knew he'd been out of line, putting the moves on her so quickly, but with her leaving as soon as the blizzard blew over, he had to act fast. Besides, he had wanted to put the considerable sparks flying between them to the test, and considering the white-hot intensity of their embrace, he wasn't sorry he had.

Noting Nora was still waiting for an answer, Sam said, "Yes, we're hooked up to the Net, as well as an information system that lets me interact with other law enforcement agencies via computer."

Nora paled slightly. "I see."

She seemed edgy, nervous. Why, he wasn't sure. Unless she was worried he was going to kiss her again? Sam stood. "Everything okay?" he asked.

"Sure, of course."

He studied her, knowing something was up. Moved closer. "I'm surprised to see you here."

"Oh, well, your grandparents wanted you to know—what with the snow coming down harder now—that they were closing the store an hour early this evening and would be going home around five. I volunteered to come over and tell you. Plus, I wanted to see a little of the town while I could still walk around."

Sam looked out the window. "It's coming down pretty good now, isn't it?"

Nora nodded. Though the brunt of the blizzard still seemed seven or eight hours away, it had really started to pick up in the past hour or so. She'd heard on the car radio that it was now snowing steadily in Kentucky, Maryland, Pennsylvania and New York state and that "record blizzard" conditions had virtually shut down all roads in the mountains of Virginia. If the forecasters were right, it would soon be that bad here, too. "I'd say we have at least four inches on the ground now," she said. And the latest forecast indicated their area of West Virginia might get sleet and ice, too. Sleet and ice knocked out power lines.

The phone rang. Sam reluctantly tore his eyes from Nora's face and picked up the receiver. "Sheriff's office." He listened, and was clearly not happy with the report on the other end. "I'll be right down," he promised, then hung up.

"Another wreck?" Nora asked curiously as he reached for his shearling coat and shrugged it on.

Sam searched for his keys and finally found them on his desk, beneath the state accident report he'd started to fill out before Nora walked in. "Worse. Domestic disturbance," he explained as Nora sauntered closer, her eyes glued to his. Sam grimaced, wishing he had time for another kiss, then continued explaining. "Clyde Redmond is down at the hardware store trying to buy a snow shovel, and his wife Charlene is there with him, pitching a fit."

Nora blinked, still not understanding. She watched as he retrieved his Stetson and adjusted the brim low across his brow. "She has something against her husband shoveling snow?"

Sam nodded, explaining, "And with good reason, since Clyde had his first heart attack two months ago, doing just that." He brushed a hand down her cheek, gave her one last lingering glance and strode out the door. "Hold down the fort here," he called over his shoulder. "I'll be right back."

THE DOOR BANGED behind Sam, leaving her very much alone.

Well, this was her chance to look around. And see

if anything from her father had come in, Nora thought as she noticed a stack of recently received faxes in the tray.

Her heart pounding, Nora picked up the stack and quickly began to look through it. The first fax sought information on a young widow from Maryland and her baby. They'd allegedly gone out to run errands early that morning and never returned home, even after it began to snow. Her in-laws were frantic for information of any kind. Next was a report on a burglary ring operating out of Charleston, West Virginia, that had hit elegant homes and various businesses all over the state. Third, came a query about a schoolteacher and seven children who had never made it to the next destination of their field trip. Could they have had car trouble or been involved in an accident? the headmistress of the Peach Blossom Academy For Young Women, wanted to know. If so, she asked that the school and the parents of the students, age 6 to 14, please be alerted ASAP. After that came a weather warning, stating that as of 4:00 p.m. that afternoon, all West Virginia freeways would be closed until further notice. On the bottom was what she had dreaded—a photo of herself in her wedding gown, and a faxed alert from Round The Clock Investigations, advising all law enforcement officials in the state to be on the lookout for Nora Hart-Kingsley.

Even worse, Nora realized with a sinking heart, a twenty-five-thousand-dollar reward was being offered for any information leading to her safe return. Twenty-five thousand dollars. When Nora thought of how far that would go to help Clover Creek get their new ambulance, it was all she could do not to shout her dismay to the world.

Nora sighed as she quickly folded the faxed report into a two-inch square and slid it into the front pocket of her jeans. Darn her father, anyway, she thought as tears filled her eyes, for publicizing what should have been a very private battle.

Darn him for refusing—just this once—to let her be and to let her make a few very important, very necessary decisions on her own.

SAM WAS GONE for fifteen minutes. Nora paced the whole time, wondering how she—a woman with a notoriously strong conscience—was going to keep from behaving like a guilty felon in his presence. Feminine intuition told her it would not be easy, but for all their sakes, she knew she had to try. She simply could not deal with her father or Geoff right now.

"Well, how'd it go?" Nora asked Sam the moment he got back, figuring it would be better to concentrate on his actions instead of her own. Because, after the way she'd been snooping around, her nerves were strung tight. "Did you get everything straightened out down at the hardware store?"

His eyes gleaming with interest, Sam studied her a long moment. "For this afternoon, anyway," he replied.

"How?" Knowing she needed something to do—and noticing that he looked chilled—she poured him a cup of coffee.

Sam gratefully accepted the mug she handed him and continued to watch her, as if some sixth sense told him something was now amiss between them that hadn't been out of sync before he left on that call.

His glance roved over her upturned face. "I got both Clyde and Charlene to agree to let me arrange for the walks around their home to be cleared by the local Boy Scout troop."

Nora watched as he lifted the mug to his lips and sipped the piping-hot brew, then turned around to pour herself a cup of coffee, too. "That's a great idea," she said cheerfully, returning to sit with him in the office.

Sam shrugged off her compliment as he, too, took a seat. "Thank goodness it worked."

Nora sipped her coffee and realized belatedly that she'd forgotten to put in cream. "Meddle often, do you?" she teased.

"I wouldn't put it that way." Sam flashed Nora a sexy grin that told her he didn't mind her joshing. "But you're right to think I don't hesitate to get involved when I can do some good."

A shiver of alarm swept through Nora. In theory, she agreed with Sam—at least when it came to keeping the peace in Clover Creek. When it came to her life, it was another matter entirely. "So you've got no qualms about interfering in someone else's personal life?" she asked.

"Not if it's for the common good," Sam conceded, looking abruptly like a man who would not hesitate to put on the pressure. "Or if it's something that needs to be done, that might not otherwise get done, because the parties involved are too stubborn to compromise, or whatever."

Nora rolled her eyes. It was all she could do to contain her exasperation. As if she didn't have enough to worry about, with her father and Geoff interfering in her life, now she had to worry about Sam, too!

She arched a dissenting brow and pushed to her feet. "That sounds like a self-serving excuse if I ever heard one," she commented as she roamed the small office restlessly.

Sam followed her with his heated gaze. "I suppose some would see it that way," he drawled.

Nora set her cup aside with a thud and whirled to face him. "But you don't."

Sam took a long sip of coffee and regarded her with a look of utter male supremacy. "Suppose just now I'd done nothing but break it up over there at the store and send them both home. Then what?"

Nora shrugged and, aware that she was the one in the hot seat, replied with as much serenity as she could muster, "They probably would've continued their argument at home."

Sam inclined his head slightly to the side. "Bingo."

Nora moved away from Sam with a shrug. "Would that have been so bad?"

Sam drained his cup, set it aside with a barely audible thunk and rolled to his feet. "In their case, probably not." Still eyeing her with a depth of male speculation that she found very disturbing, he shifted so that he stood with his feet braced slightly apart. He jammed his hands on his hips and narrowed his eyes as he continued to square off with her.

"*Unless* Clyde'd suffered another heart attack in the course of the argument, or later, while shoveling snow against Charlene's wishes," Sam continued, a serious glint coming into his eyes. "Then, I suspect none of us who witnessed the argument would ever have forgiven ourselves. Then, I imagine all of us would be wishing we'd found the courage to step in to do something."

Nora knew Sam was right. In some instances, it was a lot easier just to back off than to get personally involved. And in that sense, she could almost admire him for plunging fearlessly into the fray.

"How do you know when to draw the line?" she asked curiously, aware that his nearness had caused her heart to take up a slow, heavy beat. She tilted her head back as he rested both hands on her shoulders. "How do you know when to let something go and when to—well, meddle?"

Sam flashed her a sexy half smile that did a lot to allay her fears, and gently caressed her arms. "Depends on the stakes, I guess," he confided softly as he dropped his hands from her shoulders and moved away. "If something's at risk that can't be got back if the worst happens, like the love of a family member, then it's time for me to step in and do what I can, as a relative or a friend, as a fellow citizen, as an officer of the law, to preserve the peace and patch things up, and keep everyone happy and safe."

Nora watched him go over to the fax machine and briefly check the messages in the tray.

Guilt warred with fear. It was all she could do not

to check her pocket for the fax she had stolen, folded and hidden there.

Feigning a nonchalance she couldn't begin to feel, Nora slipped to the window and stared out at the snow falling in steady white sheets. There was nothing excessively forgiving or easy about Sam Whittaker. And she sensed that there never would be. He was who he was, take him or leave him. Trying not to think how much they had in common that way, Nora drew a steadying breath. "So, in other words, you're part cop, part social worker."

Sam shrugged and shoved his hands through his shaggy mane of hair. His gaze was completely without apology. "In a town this size, it's a necessity," he said firmly. He strode to the window and leaned one shoulder against the glass. "Someone's got to keep the peace," he stated, looking down at her.

Nora supposed that was so as their glances met and held.

"I don't want anyone losing a loved one on my watch," he confided, a hint of remorse coming into his eyes.

Nora found herself gliding toward him as their voices dropped.

"And that goes double in situations like this, where it can easily be avoided."

"I understand your reasoning," Nora remarked. *I might even think it's gallant*. She paused and bit her lip. "I suspect there are still some who think you might be going a tad overboard." *Especially if you were to try and do the same thing to or for me,* Nora thought.

Sam inclined his head slightly to the side and smiled. "I suspect you're right."

Nora sighed. "But it doesn't change your opinion about what your job here is, does it?"

"No," Sam replied, "it doesn't.

Again, their eyes locked, and Nora felt something she didn't need—or want—to feel as sparks of awareness ignited and danced all around them. He was exactly the kind of interfering, overly protective man she did not need in her life right now, and all she could think was that they didn't make men like this anymore. He was a knight in shining armor—warm, rough, and unutterably masculine...

The phone rang, breaking the spell, and jarring them apart. His eyes still locked with hers, Sam reached for the phone reluctantly. "Sheriff's office." He listened, his expression first baffled, then cheerful. "All right," Sam said finally. "We'll be right there."

"Right where?" Nora asked, wondering what was up *now*.

"My grandparents' home, two streets over," Sam confided, already handing Nora her coat. "Apparently, Gus's surprise—the pretty lady—has arrived."

Chapter Four

"Gus sent a boat!" Nora said, stunned, as she and the Whittakers gathered around the huge cabin cruiser parked in front of the Whittakers' clothing store. It was roomy enough for a dozen people and had The Pretty Lady painted on her bow.

"No wonder he wanted us to keep her 'warm and safe,'" Harold murmured, as he braved the snow pouring down from the sky to lift the protective tarp that had been tied over the top of the boat and inspect the unexpected delivery. "Snow and ice could do a lot of damage to the finish on a fine boat like this."

Clara nodded and turned up the wool collar on her coat. "We'll have to put her in the warehouse behind the store and then dry her off."

Sam nodded, and he and Harold went to tell the tractor-trailer driver where to go with his cargo. The problem of what to do with the boat settled, the three women trooped back into the warmth and shelter of the now deserted store.

"I guess this means you aren't Gus's fiancée after all," Kimberlee said sadly.

Nora flushed, embarrassed, as she inched off the

gloves she'd purchased there earlier in the afternoon. "I tried to tell you."

"We want you to stay with us anyway," Clara said as she went around the store, locking the cash registers and turning off the lights.

Nora thought of the steamy kiss Sam had already delivered. To have the two of them under the same roof? Or even have him dropping by a lot? Seeing her at all times of the day and night? "No, really," Nora told Clara and Kimberlee, "I can't possibly impose—"

Sam strode in from the back and came up to join in the conversation. He narrowed his eyes at her. "I don't think you have a choice—there are no hotels or boarding houses in Clover Creek."

"Not even a bed-and-breakfast?" Nora asked, doing her best to contain her distress. She was having trouble catching her breath, standing so near to him. And, realizing that it was ridiculous for her to be reacting that way, she stepped away. And promptly and embarrassingly backed into a display of men's shirts.

Sam reached out to steady her. "The closest hotel is back at the freeway interchange and, according to the tractor-trailer driver, those are all full now."

Deciding she had looked into his eyes long enough, Nora turned her eyes from him and addressed his grandmother.

Clara Whittaker said soothingly, "Don't worry. We've got plenty of room, and you won't be our only guest for the blizzard. Sam will be there, too."

Like that was supposed to help persuade her? Nora thought, all the more distressed.

Looking not at all displeased by the latest development, Sam explained, "My place is five miles outside town. For obvious reasons, I'm going to need to stay in town until this storm blows over, in order to do my job. Speaking of which—" Sam was interrupted by his beeper. "Looks like I've got another call." He excused himself and went off to take it in private.

"Meanwhile, we ladies have some errands to run," Clara explained.

"Can I be of help?" Nora asked.

"If you wouldn't mind waiting for Harold to finish with the boat?" Clara replied with a smile.

"Not at all."

That settled, Kimberlee went to the market to get extra milk and bread. Clara went off to the post office to collect the mail. Nora went out to the warehouse to watch as the truck driver and his assistant began unloading the *Pretty Lady* from the trailer bed.

"What's up?" Harold asked Sam, when he joined them a couple of minutes later. "Nora said you had a call."

Sam nodded, his concern evident. "That was Boots McKinney. His golden retriever, Clementine, is missing. He let her out about four this afternoon, and she hasn't come back. Boots is out of his mind with worry."

Sam turned to Nora, explaining, "Boots is still recovering from a broken hip and can't go out and look for Clem himself."

"He must be frantic."

"And then some," Sam conceded grimly. He

sighed and shook his head, his frustration at the situation evident. ''I have a feeling Clem's in trouble, too. Otherwise, she would've been back, 'cause she's absolutely devoted to Boots.''

His mouth set determinedly, Sam buttoned his coat. ''I'm going out to look for Clementine, and do what I can for Boots.''

Nora looked at the sky. Snow was still coming down with ever-increasing intensity. It would be dark in another hour or two. She hated to think of any pet out on a night like this, and knew Sam could probably use some assistance, since he was obviously a one-man law enforcement unit; besides, if they didn't find the beloved retriever before darkness set in, Clementine probably wouldn't survive the night.

Nora looked at Sam, her worry over the possibility of him making another pass at her subdued by this greater emergency. ''Do you need help?'' she asked.

Sam nodded, his mind solely on the task ahead. ''I'd appreciate it. So would Boots, I'm sure.''

IF ANYTHING, Sam thought, the seventy-nine-year-old Boots McKinney was even more frantic by the time he and Nora showed up at his rustic cabin in the woods. ''Sam, you've got to find her,'' Boots said.

I'll do my best, Sam thought. Although in this weather, with the snow coming down harder with each moment that passed, and darkness descending more swiftly than usual, it was hard to guarantee results, especially when his two deputies were on other calls. ''Any idea which way she was headed when she took off?'' Sam asked the retiree.

"No, and she's never been gone this long when it's this cold out." Boots gripped either side of his metal walker until his knuckles turned white. "I keep thinking I hear her barking, but it's so faint, I can't be sure—" Boots stopped, too choked up to continue.

Nora moved in beside Sam and looked at Boots kindly. "Which way do you think the barking is coming from?" she asked gently.

"Back behind the house, fairly deep in the woods. She may have been on the scent of something." Boots paused to wipe his eyes as he told Nora, "Retrievers are hunting dogs, you know."

Sam cast a look over his shoulder at the dark, silent woods. Anxious to get started before any more time elapsed, he took Nora's elbow and led her toward the door. "We'll let you know what we find," Sam told Boots over his shoulder.

Flashlight in hand, Sam and Nora bundled up against the blowing snow and frigid air and headed off. As they trudged through what appeared to be six or so inches of accumulated snow, Sam took a dog whistle out of his pocket and began to blow into it, emitting a pitch that was too high for them to hear. To his relief, they soon heard the faint but unmistakable sound of a dog. Unfortunately, Clementine was not barking, but whimpering.

"She sounds hurt," Nora said worriedly as they topped a steep hill and stood looking down into an even steeper incline, peppered with huge pine trees.

My feelings exactly, Sam thought, as he flashed his light down the ravine. Clementine was at the very bottom. When she saw them, she tried to leap forward, only to let out a high-pitched yelp.

"Her tail's trapped beneath that fallen pine tree," Nora said.

"If it's only her tail, she's probably not hurt."

Carefully they made their way down the snow-slick incline. More than once, they nearly lost their footing, but working together and holding on to trees, they both managed to stay upright until they reached the bottom of the steep incline.

Clementine whimpered pitifully as they approached.

"Hello, girl…" Nora knelt in front of her and held out a gloved hand, palm up, for her to sniff. Talking softly all the while, Nora petted the overgrown pup gently on the head and rubbed behind her ears, while Sam went around to investigate the downed tree that had landed on her tail and trapped her on the snowy slope for the past six hours or so.

"I don't think we're going to be able to lift it," he announced grimly, "but I think we can free her if we dig some of the snow and leaves out just beneath her tail."

Together, Sam and Nora worked on opposite sides. Short minutes later, Clementine let out a joyful yelp and scrambled free. She landed against Sam's chest, and he caught her in his arms, petting her softly and crooning to her. "Easy, girl, you're all right now, you're all right."

Nora grinned from ear to ear as she checked out Clementine's tail, which did indeed seem to be fine. "We did it!" she exclaimed happily.

Sam looked at Nora, unable to help but think what a good team they made, as he held out a hand and helped her to her feet. "We sure did," he said with a grin, thinking that despite all the extra work the blizzard was sending his way, it had also sent someone very special. And for that he was very glad.

Nora dusted the snow off her knees. Then reached up and brushed off his shoulders, too. "Guess we better get back to Mr. McKinney," she said, almost shyly.

Sam nodded. Whatever it was he was feeling, it was clear that Nora was feeling it, too.

Together, the two of them and the dog made their way carefully up the slope and back to the rustic cabin.

Wary of the changing weather's effects on the roads and concerned about their ability to return to town, Sam and Nora stayed just long enough to see that Boots and his beloved pet were reunited and carry in a new load of wood for Boots's fireplace and then were on their way.

Though they'd only been away an hour, Sam's truck was already covered with several inches of snow. He helped her up into the passenger seat, went around and started the engine, then got back out and cleared away the snow that had accumulated on the windows with a long brush. Finished, he hopped back in. Nora was huddled in her seat, shivering in spite of the lukewarm air blowing out of the vents. She bit her lip worriedly as she studied the snow-covered road. "Are you going to be able to drive in this?"

Sam reassured her. "No problem. The snow's still

pretty soft, and my wheelbase is high enough off the ground to maneuver through it.''

Tomorrow morning may be another story, though, he said to himself. Depending on how hard the rest of the coast got hit, Nora could be stuck here for days before she was able to get back on the freeway again. That thought didn't bother him as much as it should. Maybe because he sensed that she needed his help.

Sam put the truck in four-wheel drive and carefully maneuvered his way out of the McKinney driveway. He drove slowly and cautiously through the snow; nevertheless, his truck slid several times in the first half mile or so. Each time it did, Nora held on all the tighter.

Sam knew they'd make it to their destination, though the normal ten-minute drive back into Clover Creek was bound to take two or three times as long. He reached over and squeezed her hand. ''Hang on. We're going to get there.''

Nora's fingers curled tightly beneath his. ''I know. You're doing an excellent job of driving, by the way.''

''Thanks.'' Not about to take any chances with his precious passenger, Sam withdrew his hand from hers and put it back on the steering wheel. ''I've had a lot of practice driving in snow and ice.''

''Me too,'' Nora said, watching the road as intently as he was. She jerked in a breath as the wheels on the truck temporarily lost traction and they skidded a little to the right, then relaxed slightly as they got back on course. Sam wished he could pull over to the side of the road and hold Nora in his arms and comfort her, but he knew the best thing to do was get them both back to town before the roads got any worse.

Nora sighed heavily. "Ever wish you didn't have to deal with it and could live somewhere warm and sunny year-round?"

The answer to that was easy, Sam thought. "No, West Virginia is home. I haven't always lived here—I went to college in Kentucky and spent seven years working for the Chicago Police Department—but now that I'm back, I plan to stay."

"You don't mind that Clover Creek is so small—populationwise?" Nora asked, holding her hands out to the warm air flowing through the heat vents.

Sam only saw one problem there—the close attention paid by the small town might put a crimp in his attempts to romance the woman beside him. He didn't want anything or anyone getting in the way of that. "It's sometimes like living in a fishbowl," Sam acknowledged sagely, "with everyone minding what is going on in everyone else's life, but when you consider it's done out of love and not mean-spiritedness, it's not so bad."

"The lack of privacy might bother me," Nora allowed with a frown, before her voice turned wistful once again. "But everything else...the close-knit ties...the safe, bucolic atmosphere of small-town life...seems very appealing. Before I decided to marry Geoff, I was considering getting out of the rat race altogether and living in a small town."

This was a surprise. "How did your family feel about that?" Sam asked curiously, turning his attention back to the road. The snow was coming down even harder now, and the darkness of night was now a factor. He figured they had ten yards' visibility, at best.

Nora was silent a long moment. "Both my father and Geoff were adamantly against it," she said softly at last. "My father wanted me in the family business, right alongside he and Geoff."

Geoff again. Sam was beginning to dislike that guy a lot. "But you weren't interested?" Sam probed, as they passed the Culpepper farm's mailbox. Only two more miles and they would be in town again, he thought, relieved.

"No." Nora's voice was firm. "The restaurant business is not really for me."

So what was? Sam wondered as they crested a hill and the driveway and mailbox of another farm came into view. "Any chance you'll go back to the New York City advertising world where you met my brother Gus?"

Nora shrugged as they reached the edge of town. "I thought about it for about five minutes after I called off my wedding, and then I decided to go back to my original plan and do something completely different. Drop out of the world I knew, settle somewhere new and work in a business of my own."

"Those are some mighty big changes you're talking about." Sam wasn't sure she knew how big.

"I know," Nora said seriously.

Sam parked in front of the sheriff's office. For the first time all day, Main Street was completely deserted. There was not a single other vehicle in sight.

Sam cut the engine and turned toward Nora. "How do you think your father is going to react to your decision to drop out and relocate?"

Nora regarded Sam as if he were a chastising sibling. "I imagine my father will be surprised, but then—" Nora sighed reluctantly "—life is full of surprises. And they always—*always*—hit you when you least expect it."

That was certainly true, Sam thought as he circled around to help her down from the passenger seat. They walked back inside the sheriff's office. As adults, they were entitled to do as they pleased with their lives. But that did not mean they should also disregard the feelings of those close to them, out of pique or anything else.

Sam shut the door behind them. He pivoted toward her, and his eyes lasered down into hers as he said, "Speaking of loved ones, Nora—do yours know where you are?"

This, Nora hadn't expected. Worse, the faxed message that she'd illegally intercepted from Sam's office was burning a hole in Nora's pocket. What would Sam do if he knew her father was searching for her at this moment? Would he call her dad? Nora wondered uneasily, trying not to think how much his mere presence was undoing her.

"Um, actually—"

His head lifted. He speared her with a gaze that raised her pulse another notch and pinned her to the spot. His eyes really were an incredible mixture of gold and brown.

"Have you telephoned them to let them know

you're okay?'' Sam persisted, edging close enough for Nora to inhale the scent of his cologne.

Nora backed away, wishing he didn't look and smell so good. ''Not yet.''

Sam lounged against his desk. ''You can use my phone, if you'd like.''

Nora forced a tight smile. ''Thanks, but...no.''

He regarded her steadily, seeming to disagree with her decision to keep her family in the dark about where she was for even a moment longer.

''That fiancé of yours hurt you badly, didn't he?''

Nora shrugged and regarded him in the same bold manner in which he was regarding her. ''Both my father and Geoff did.''

''So in other words,'' Sam retorted mildly, ''you have no compunction about dishing it right back at them, by not calling and letting them know you're all right.''

Nora flushed guiltily, knowing that Sam was right. Both her father and Geoff had probably been very hurt and humiliated by the way she'd run off. But it was no worse than what they'd done to her, keeping her in the dark about the dowry. Like this was the Dark Ages, for heaven's sake! She dug in her heels stubbornly and refused to give ground. ''If I call them, they'll want me to come back home.''

''That makes sense,'' he said as his gaze swept the snow-dusted length of her before returning to her face. ''It sounds like you have a lot to straighten out.''

Nora's breasts rose and fell with each agitated breath she took. ''They'll also try to take advantage of me again, in a million and one ways.''

Sam shrugged, as if that were hardly the point. "So don't let them."

If only she could wave a magic wand and make that happen! Nora balled her hands into fists and struggled to get herself together. "It's not that simple."

Sam straightened. His sensual mouth tightened with a disapproval that he made no effort to hide. "Yes, Nora, it is."

Nora pivoted away from him and stalked to the bulletin board with the Wanted posters. "You don't understand." *You don't know how long and hard I've already tried.*

He closed the distance between them wordlessly, put his hands on her shoulders and turned her around to face him. "Then explain it to me so I do," he urged compassionately.

Nora swallowed and looked up at him, knowing she wanted him to understand and even approve of her, even if she couldn't yet tell him everything. "Sam, I—"

Without warning, there was a loud, crackling pop, and then everything descended into darkness.

"WHAT HAPPENED?" Nora asked, trembling. Frightened, she reached out for Sam.

He tucked her against him, then moved to the window and looked out. As he'd suspected, the entire town was dark. "The electricity just went off," he told Nora as he picked up a flashlight from the table in the corner and switched it on. "Some power lines were probably knocked out due to the ferocity of the blizzard. Maybe the phone and cable, too.''

Sam picked up the phone. As he had feared, it was also dead.

"How long before they're fixed?" Nora shivered and stayed even closer.

Sam shrugged. "The power lines will most likely be down for the duration of the snowstorm. It'll probably be days before the phone service is restored to everyone."

Nora sighed and backed away from his arms. "So for the moment, anyway, you're completely cut off from the outside world, then?"

She sounded more pleased about that than she ought to be, Sam thought. Probably because, through no fault of her own, she'd just won herself a reprieve from having to deal with whatever it was she was running from. "We can still use our shortwave radios," Sam told her, and tried not to feel bereft about the fact that he no longer held her in his arms. "We won't be able to pick up much with our transistors, though. Reception in this area is poor, due to all the interference from the mountains." He surveyed the office and found everything in order. "Might as well close up shop here."

"Can you do that?" Nora asked, staying close by his side. "I thought all police departments were open twenty-four hours a day."

Sam tried not to think about how much he liked having Nora with him, or how helpful she'd been out on that last call or how pretty she looked in a wedding gown. "In weather like this, even the criminals stay home and snuggle up by the fire.'' Sam's blood warmed as he thought about doing just that with Nora. ''Besides, now that it's past four o'clock, I am officially off duty. Clover Creek also employs two deputies. They'll be taking the 4:00 p.m. to midnight and midnight to 8:00 a.m. shifts.'' He glanced at his watch. ''In fact, Hank's probably over at the fire station, checking in with them now.''

''Still...with all the snow-related emergencies...'' Nora hesitated. ''Don't you think we ought to wait here just a little while longer, in case you are needed?''

Using the flashlight, Sam went around locking up. Outside, there was a good eight inches of snow on the ground, and more falling. ''If I'm needed for backup, someone will call me on the shortwave radio. Besides, we can't stay here. This building has no fireplace. We'll have to go over to my grandparents' home.'' Sam wreathed an arm about her shoulders and led her toward the door.

''Do they have a fireplace?'' Nora asked.

''Most of the rooms do,'' Sam told her as he escorted her outside to his truck. The snow had started coming down in thick, heavy sheets. No wonder the power was out. It was a struggle to walk in the driving wind. He drove her to Whittakers, and helped her get her suitcase from her car. Realizing it was impossible to dig her car out at that point, they decided to leave it where it was for the time being, and then headed over to Sam's grandparents' home. Once again, the roads were hard to maneuver, even in a vehicle with a high wheelbase and four-wheel drive, and Sam's truck fishtailed left and right down the street, losing traction as often as it gained it.

THE WHITTAKER HOME was a charming old Victorian, surrounded by snow-covered trees. Looking as if it had come straight out of a Norman Rockwell painting, the rambling three-story home was painted a soft slate blue and had white shutters and a glossy black door. A wraparound veranda circled the entire first floor, a white picket fence the yard.

Wood smoke curled from chimneys on either end of the home, and the windows were lit with the soft glow of candle-lanterns. Inside, the home was just as warm and cozy. Antiques were polished to a high gleam, chintz-covered furniture was deep and overstuffed and colorful rugs decorated the beautiful wood floors.

While Sam carried in the suitcase she'd meant to take on her honeymoon, Nora paused in front of a collection of family photos on the grand piano in the living room. As Sam joined her, she nodded at a photo of Sam, Kimberlee, Gus and what appeared to be his parents, at a backyard barbecue. They were gathered around a grill, cooking together and laughing, obviously having a great time. "Are these your parents?"

Sam nodded, his expression a mix of affection and grief. He picked up the photo and cradled it gently in his hand. "This was taken the summer before my parents died. It was the last time we were all together."

Nora's heart went out to him. Having lost her own

mother, she knew how much a parent's death hurt. "What happened?" she asked softly.

Sam untied his tie with one hand and loosened the first button of his shirt. "They got caught in a fierce winter rainstorm, while they were driving up to Chicago to see me. A tractor-trailer crossed the median and hit their car and several others head-on. Everyone involved in the crash was killed instantly."

"I'm sorry." Nora turned away from the photo and looked into his eyes. "That must've been tough."

Sam nodded, admitting, "It was. Is. I wish we'd spent more time together while we had the chance. I wish I'd come home that last Christmas, instead of working. If I had, they probably would have waited until later in the spring to come see me, instead of risking a trip in dubious weather in late February. Intellectually, of course, I know the accident could have happened anywhere, anytime. But in here—" Sam shook his head sadly and pointed to his heart "—I think I'm always going to regret the opportunities lost to us. The times I didn't come home. The holidays I missed. The sheer physical distance I put between us, for the sake of my career. 'Cause, looking back, there isn't anything I wouldn't trade to have my folks here with me now. And I know Kimberlee, Gus, my grandparents, all feel the same."

Which was probably, Nora thought compassionately, why he was so gung ho about her contacting her own family.

Sam nodded and put the photo back in its place. "We better see where everyone is," he said.

"Gran, Granddad, Kimberlee?" Sam called, as

they moved through the spacious downstairs and ended up in a large country kitchen.

"Here's a note," Nora said, picking it up from the counter. "And it's addressed to the two of us."

"'Dear Sam and Nora,'" Nora read out loud. "'The three of us are going door-to-door to make sure all our elderly neighbors are set for the night with flashlights and batteries or candles and fires in their fireplaces. We'll be back soon. If you get home before we do, maybe you could build the fires in the third-floor bedrooms for you and Nora. Love, Gran.'"

"Well, we've got our orders," Sam said. They donned their coats and gloves again, grabbed two canvas wood carriers and braved the cold winter wind and snow to trudge out into the backyard. Each of them brought in an armful of wood, and then Sam led the way up the stairs. "You and I will both be sleeping on the third floor."

Nora pushed the mental image of that aside. "Where will everyone else be sleeping?" she asked.

"Second." As they passed through that, Sam gave her a brief tour via candle-lantern, showing her the master bedroom where his grandparents slept, Kimberlee's room, a sewing room for his grandmother and a study for his grandfather. All were lovingly decorated and maintained. "The third floor has two more bedrooms, a shared, connecting bath and separate enclosed storage area," Sam said matter-of-factly as they carried the wood up the last of the stairs.

Candle-lanterns had been lit up there, too, and they illuminated the entire third floor with a cozy glow that Nora found far too romantic for comfort.

Sam's only going to be one room away, Nora thought as she surveyed the room at the head of the stairs, and a shiver of sensual awareness ghosted down her spine.

Unhappy with the sensual direction of her thoughts, she forced herself to concentrate on the specifics of her surroundings.

The furniture was heavy and masculine. A roomy double bed, decorated with a tartan plaid spread, filled the center of the room. A police radio sat on the nightstand beside the bed. "This is the room you usually take when you stay over?" Nora guessed as Sam set his wood into the bucket beside the grate and then gallantly took charge of the wood she was carrying, too.

"Right. Towels and so on are in here." He pointed to a small linen closet as they passed the bathroom they would share. "And this is where you'll be," he said, leading the way past the aforementioned storage area door, down the short hall and into another superbly decorated room.

It, too, featured a comfortable-looking double bed, with a masculine paisley spread. Intending to tell Sam what a lovely home his grandparents had, Nora turned around and nearly bumped into him. Startled by his nearness, she moved back. He held his ground. As Nora looked into his face, she could tell he wanted to kiss her again. What surprised her was that she wanted him to kiss her, too. And now that Sam knew for certain she was not his brother's fiancée, there was nothing to stop him from making a move on her, nothing except the fact that his grandparents and Kimberlee could return and walk in on them at any time....

Sam broke the staring match first. "Guess we better get those fires going," he drawled, looking not nearly as chagrined by the temptation to dally as she was. "Can you handle the one in here?" he asked.

"Sure," Nora fibbed. Although her father had never wanted her to fiddle with the fireplaces at home—he considered it a man's job and preferred to do it himself—she had watched him build a fire plenty of times. How hard could it be?

Plenty hard, as it turned out. The logs were more unwieldy to arrange in the grate than she'd figured, but she experimented until she had successfully arranged them in a crosswise fashion, so that the air could circulate between them, then stuffed rolled newspaper in the cracks. Remembering the stolen fax in her pocket, she glanced around to make sure the coast was clear, saw that Sam was still busy building his own fire, then rolled it up cylinder-style and stuck it in between the logs, too.

Finished, she lit the fire and watched both the fax and the newspaper take flame. Satisfied, she stepped back to watch the evidence of her theft blacken, inch by incriminating inch. Only when it had almost finished burning did she realize that something else was amiss. Was it her imagination, or was her room beginning to smell a little too smoky for comfort?

Sam came rushing over. He took one look at the haze in the air and demanded, "Did you open the flue?"

Nora whirled toward him. "The what?" she countered, confused.

"Oh, damn," Sam swore, rolling his eyes. "Open a window, quick," he ordered. While Nora rushed to comply, Sam grabbed a small fire-retardant rug from in front of the fireplace and smothered the flames, knocking a roll of the still-burning newspaper out onto the brick hearth in the process. Using the shovel and andiron, Sam beat the remaining flames out on the hearth. Too late, Nora realized it wasn't only newspaper he had knocked onto the floor.

Fearing it was what she'd been trying to discretely burn, Nora reached for the half-burned fax with feigned casualness. "I'll get that."

Sam beat her to the punch. "Your hands will get all sooty. What the—" He paused to identify a smudged but otherwise unharmed corner of the fax paper. The photo of Nora and the accompanying message had been burned away. But half the date and part of the phone number where the fax had originated were still legible on the corner of the page. Clearly, Nora thought, seeing it through Sam's eyes, this was no newspaper.

Sam turned to Nora, his suspicion evident. "How did this get in here?" he demanded.

Chapter Five

Nora hitched in a breath, her heart hammering in her chest and her mouth unaccountably dry, as she snatched it back and wadded what was left of the burned fax into a sooty wad that effectively prevented further analysis.

"I put it in there," she announced haughtily, realizing that since she'd been caught red-handed, she had no choice but to tell Sam as much of the truth as she dared. She tossed her head defiantly. "I'd been carrying it around in my pocket, and I didn't want it anymore."

Sam's glance roved over her upturned face. He was clearly trying to contain his suspicion, though not quite succeeding. "What was it?" he asked softly, as she tossed it carelessly back into the grate.

Nora glowered at him. She could feel the blood rushing to her cheeks, even as she struggled to get a handle on her soaring emotions. "A message from someone who works for my father that has to do with me." She spun away from him and stalked away. Pivoting smartly on her heel, she folded her arms in front of her and whirled to face him. "Satisfied?"

With a sinking heart, she realized that it didn't appear so, but Sam never had a chance to reply. The sound of a door slamming downstairs had them springing farther apart.

"Yoo-hoo! Sam! Nora! We're home."

"We better go down," Nora said, wanting the emotional inquisition to end.

"In a minute," Sam decreed, then paused to shout an acknowledgment to his grandparents, indicating that they'd be downstairs directly. His eyes on hers, he continued, "First, I want to open the flue."

While Nora watched, Sam leaned into the fireplace and swiftly accomplished what she had foolishly failed to do. Realizing that the smoke in the room had cleared—if not the lingering tension between the two of them—Nora sprinted over and closed the window. Sam rebuilt and relit the fire, leaving the wadded-up fax where it lay.

Moments later, satisfied that all was going as it should, and no more smoke was entering the room, he stood and dusted off his hands. "We better wash up," he said.

Her head held high, her body tingling all over, she brushed past Sam. They washed up wordlessly, then headed swiftly down the stairs. Sam kept eyeing her, but said nothing more about the fax. Nora wondered whether he knew the fax had come from his office, or just suspected it had. The partial phone number, the date and the time were dead giveaways. The question was, how much of it had he actually been able to read before she snatched the offending evidence of her crime away?

There was no clue on his face as Nora and Sam entered the homey kitchen. "All the neighbors settled for the night?" Sam asked, helping Kimberlee set the table for dinner, while his grandmother and grandfather brought over steaming bowls of minestrone and plates of thick, hearty sandwiches.

Though they did not have electricity, Nora noted as she took the seat Harold indicated that the Whittakers' large gas stove appeared to be working just fine.

Clara nodded. "What about you two? Did you start the fires in the guest rooms' fireplaces?"

Those and more, Nora thought, aware that she was still tingling from the close proximity to Sam. And he hadn't even touched her, or made another attempt to kiss her.

Sam nodded, his own thoughts as mysterious as the expression on his face. He smiled at his grandmother. "With enough quilts on the beds, we should all be okay for the night," he said.

"Okay but cold," Kimberlee said, as the rest of the family sat down at the table and spread their napkins across their laps.

As they began eating, talk turned to their neighbors. Clara and Harold filled Sam and Nora in on how everyone was faring, given the sudden lack of electricity.

"Thank heavens I won't have to endure this hardship much longer," Kimberlee eventually exclaimed with relief as the meal drew to a close and Clara got up to bring a pot of stove-brewed coffee to the table.

"Next winter I'll be in Chicago, where I won't be

without electricity and phone and cable every time
there's a little itty-bitty storm,'' Kimberlee continued
wistfully.

Nora watched as Sam and his grandparents exchanged concerned looks as a dessert of coffee and
chocolate-chip pound cake was served.

Whatever was going on, Nora noted, Clara and
Harold seemed to be leaving it up to Sam to take
charge of the situation.

''This is more than 'a little itty-bitty storm.''' Sam
nodded at the bay windows, where they could see
snow still coming down at an astounding rate. ''It's
the snowstorm of the century, and as much as I hate
to bring it up yet again, I thought we'd settled this,''
he reminded his younger sister. ''There is no way I
am letting you go to college in Chicago just so you
can be near your boyfriend.''

Kimberlee's chin thrust out, and her expression
turned pouty. ''You are not my parent, Sam,'' she
growled.

''But I am your legal guardian.''

Nora noted that Sam did not look as if he were
enjoying this confrontation any more than Kimberlee
was.

Kimberlee put her fork down with a clatter. She
sent pleading glances to Clara and Harold. ''Gran,
Granddad, talk to him!''

Clara looked at Kimberlee. ''I'm sorry, honey. I'm
afraid your granddad and I agree with your brother
on this. You shouldn't pick a college just because
your boyfriend is already going there.''

''You go to college to prepare for a career,'' Harold told her gently. "And since your boyfriend's college has no nursing program—"

"So I'll do that later!" Kimberlee said. Eyes sparkling, she shoved her unfinished dessert aside. "I don't care what I study now!"

Sam sighed, exasperated. He leaned forward as he gently tried to reason with his younger sister. "You're missing the point, Kimberlee."

"No, you're missing the point, Sam!" Kimberlee shot right back angrily, pushing her chair away from the table with an earsplitting screech. "I'm going to college in Chicago, and that's that!"

"Over my dead body!" Sam said, completely losing patience.

"That may just have to be!" Kimberlee shouted as mortified tears streamed down her face. Shooting another look of abject misery at everyone at the table, she sprang to her feet and stormed out of the room.

Silence fell in the aftermath of Kimberlee's dramatic departure. Sam and his grandparents looked miserable. Nora wanted to find somewhere to hide. "I think I'll go upstairs and get settled in," Nora said tactfully, deciding they needed time alone.

"Let us know if you need anything," Clara murmured, distracted, as Sam and his grandparents helped themselves to more coffee.

Nora left them finishing their dessert. As she reached the second floor, she heard anguished sobs coming from Kimberlee's room. On impulse, hoping she could help, she followed the sound. Kimberlee's bedroom door was ajar. She had thrown herself across her bed.

Nora paused in front of the portal. She knew this was none of her business. But she never had been able to turn away from someone in need. And from the sound of that sobbing, Kimberlee needed someone to talk with, someone who was removed enough from the situation to be objective. Someone like her, who knew firsthand what it was like to have your family not understand you.

She knocked. Kimberlee looked up and beckoned her in.

"I'm sorry you're having such a rough time," Nora said softly as she sat down on the edge of Kimberlee's bed.

Kimberlee shoved her golden-brown hair from her eyes. "It's all Sam's fault!" Kimberlee said, fuming. "You heard him down there. He's just so unreasonable."

Protective, Nora thought, and maybe that wasn't such a bad thing. "Do you want to talk about it?" she asked gently.

"I guess I might as well." Kimberlee sniffed, sitting up. She reached for a tissue and blew her nose. "I'm in love. I'm so in love I can't stand it. Only no one in the family supports me on this," she continued, wiping her eyes. "You heard Sam and my grandparents. They didn't even want me to apply to the University of Chicago! I had to cough up the application fee myself. And it wasn't cheap! But you know what?" Kimberlee asked angrily. "I did it anyway. And you know what else? I'm going to get in. 'Cause I've got the grades and the extracurriculars and the SAT scores to get admitted."

Kimberlee barely paused to take a breath as she blotted the tears from her face. "You know what the worst thing is? I almost had my grandparents' support on this. And then Sam heard about it and found out U of C didn't have a nursing program and started interfering, and now he's convinced my grandparents I shouldn't go there at all!"

Nora sifted through the emotion to the facts underneath. "Do you want to be a nurse?"

"Well, yes," Kimberlee admitted, flushing, "but that can wait. My love for Kenny can't. And before you even say it, I know what you're thinking." Kimberlee held up a hand, stop-sign-fashion. "I'm very young. But that doesn't mean I can't love someone, 'cause I do."

"Maybe if you talked to Sam again," Nora suggested gently, "and told him how much this all means to you—"

"I already have. He won't listen." Kimberlee threw herself into Nora's arms and began to sob again as if her heart would break. "I just don't know what I'm going to do, Nora! I can't be away from my boyfriend for three more years, till he graduates. It's too hard. I miss him too much. And if Sam and my grandparents make me, well, I'll just die!"

"How is she?" Sam asked an hour later from the open doorway of Nora's room.

Nora looked up from her perch in front of the fireplace. She was glad Sam had sought her out; she'd been hoping they could talk about this. "She's still pretty upset." Nora relayed hesitantly, not sure how blunt she needed to be in order to help. "I imagine she'll cry herself to sleep tonight."

"Better here and now than next year in Chicago." Sam sighed regretfully as he brought a quilt in and laid it on the end of the brass bed where Nora would be sleeping.

Nora studied the ruggedly handsome lines of Sam's face, aware that her heart was beating double-time now that he was near again. "You don't think she and her boyfriend are meant to be together long-term?" she queried softly.

Sam's frown deepened. "I think she's too young to know, and in the meantime should be preparing for her career." Sam crossed the room in two long strides, then hunkered down in front of the fire with Nora. To Nora's relief, he seemed as eager to talk privately as she. "Although I don't suspect Kimberlee will ever see it that way."

Nora was silent, thinking. She approved of the fact that Sam loved and cared for his sister and was trying to do the right thing on Kim's behalf. She didn't approve of the autocratic way he was handling the dispute. It reminded her too much of her own father, and the way he had handled things with Nora when she was eighteen. "Shouldn't it be Kimberlee's decision, where she goes to college?" Nora asked gently, trying to play intermediary.

"Sure, provided she's going there for the right reason." Sam sat facing Nora, his back to the hearth, one leg raised and bent at the knee. "But we both know she's not."

Unable to dispute that, Nora fell silent. She wished

she could do something to circumvent the misery they were both in.

"I'm doing what I think is best for my sister," Sam said stiffly, defensively.

Nora reached out and covered Sam's hand with hers. "I know you are," she said.

He turned his palm so it lay flat beneath her hand, and tightened his fingers on hers. "But...?"

Nora shrugged, knowing she felt strangely at peace, just sitting there with him, and that—whether Sam liked it or not—this had to be said. "Kimberlee's right about one thing. You're not listening to her. You're just writing off her feelings because she is so young."

Sam's shook his head in mute self-remonstration. His whole body was stiff with accumulated tension and worry. Making a concerted effort to relax, he tilted his head back, and his hair glowed a soft golden-brown in the firelight. He cupped her hand between the two of his and stroked it gently with his thumbs. "What would you have me do?"

Nora hitched in a breath at the thrill his touch engendered. As his grip on her tightened and the tempo of the stroking picked up, the feeling intensified. Tremors started deep inside her. Lower still, there was a persistent ache. "Look for a compromise with her."

Sam regarded Nora with respect. "You really feel for her, don't you?"

"Let's just say I recall all too well what it's like, knowing that what I want for me is more important than what others want for me."

His sensual lips tightened in frustration. "Kim knows we love her."

"But you don't understand her, Sam," Nora persisted. "If you did, you'd know how to talk to her without this turning into an all-out war."

Sam sighed, dropped her hand and stood. "So what are you suggesting I do?" he asked as he paced restlessly back and forth.

Nora stood and moved to the window, where they could see snow still coming down at an alarming rate. She touched his shoulder gently and felt the strong muscles tense beneath her hand. "Try looking at things from her point of view. Try putting yourself in her place. Remember what you felt at her age, what you felt the first time you fell in love...." *What I'm feeling now*, Nora thought. "And then listen to her with your heart this time, instead of just your head."

The only problem was, Sam thought, he wasn't sure he'd ever been in love. In lust, absolutely. But in love to the point where he'd be willing to give up anything and everything just to be with another person? That, he didn't know about.

Sam turned to Nora, wishing he'd met and dated her years ago, wishing he could date her now, instead of just harboring her temporarily from the storm. Maybe then he'd have the kind of lasting, loving marriage his grandparents and parents had had.

"You look confused," Nora teased, suddenly seeming to be able to read his mind all too well. "And more than that, a little wistful."

"A normal state," Sam explained wryly as their glances met and held, "when it comes to examining my feelings under a microscope." *A normal state, when I'm this close to you.*

The shortwave radio crackled in the other room. Sam frowned at the interruption. He had known that peace would not prevail for long with weather like this, even with two deputies working overtime. Sam excused himself and went to answer the call. "Problem?" Nora asked, when he returned.

Sam nodded as he pinned on his badge and knotted his tie. He wished he didn't have to leave Nora; he had been enjoying their time together. "I've got to get a message to a woman who doesn't speak anything but German. Unfortunately, I don't speak her language, and the German teacher at the high school lives on a farm ten miles out." Sam sighed and shook his head at the enormity of the problem facing him. "So I've got to figure out who might know enough to get the message across and be willing to help me out," he continued, lacing up his boots.

Nora was already hunting around for her own boots. "I could probably help you out."

"You speak German?"

"And French and Spanish. My father insisted I become fluent in several languages."

"Well, that's one problem solved," Sam said cheerfully. "Now for the second." He looked out the third-floor window. Judging from the height of the snow gathering on the eaves, there was about nine inches and counting. Which meant it would be even higher on the ground, in places where it had accumulated in drifts. Not to mention the problem they'd have stomping through it. He turned back to Nora and accompanied her down two flights of stairs. "Have you ever strapped on snowshoes?"

"No, but I'm sure I could learn," Nora told him confidently as they went to the coat tree in the front hall and retrieved their coats.

Sam reached over to help her into her parka. The silk of her hair brushed against his wrist, and the light floral scent of her perfume teased his senses. It was all he could do not to fantasize about what it would be like to have her around every day.

"How far is it?" Nora asked as she removed a tube of lip balm from her pocket and brushed some across her lips.

Sam forced his gaze away from her soft pink lips. *This was no time to be thinking about kissing her again.*

He watched as Nora threaded her hands through her hair and lifted the glossy bittersweet-chocolate length of it out of her collar, where it had gotten tangled with her scarf. "Not far," he said, a little rustily, reaching a hand out to help her. "It's in town, about three blocks over from here," he said, as their hands collided. He pulled the scarf away from her collar, and she tucked her hair behind her ear. "I'd drive, but—the way it's drifting up to a foot and a half in places—it looks too high to get my truck through. And the snowplows won't be out to clear the streets again until morning."

Nora shrugged as she buttoned the toggle buttons on her parka. Sam was pleased to note that she looked game for anything. "Then on foot it is," she said cheerfully as Sam shrugged into his own coat, hat and gloves—then helped them both strap on snowshoes.

With them thus outfitted, Sam opened the door.

If it had been snowing before, it was a blizzard now. Bitterly cold. With snow coming down in daunting white sheets. He wasn't afraid of getting lost—he could walk these streets blindfolded. But he knew they'd be chilled to the bone by the time they got back. He turned to Nora, giving her one last chance to back out. "You're sure you want to do this?" he asked seriously.

Nora's chin set determinedly as she tugged on her gloves and hat and wrapped her wool scarf up to her chin. "Positive. Let's go."

The wind was in their faces as they headed out, which made conversation all but impossible. Sam held on to Nora's arm as they trooped through the snow, the beam of a single flashlight showing the way. Fifteen minutes later, they were there. Sam had barely knocked once when the door opened.

"Frau Heidtmann?" he asked.

The older woman nodded and, tears streaming down her face, began speaking in rapid German.

As Sam had expected would be the case, he didn't understand a word of what she was saying. He looked to Nora for translation as Frau Heidtmann ushered them in. "She wants to know if you've brought her bad news about her daughter and son-in-law," Nora explained.

Sam shook his head. "Tell her they are both fine. They got caught in the storm on the way home, and are staying in a hotel in Charleston."

Nora repeated the message in rapid German. The older woman practically collapsed with relief. Her hand pressed to her heart, she spoke again. Nora smiled, and put her hand on the woman's shoulder, and consoled her with a flow of German words that seemed to work wonders.

After a moment, the woman composed herself, and asked something else in German. Nora turned to Sam. "Apparently, her daughter is expecting a baby in April. Did you hear how the ultrasound test went?"

"All is well there, too," Sam said.

Nora repeated the information. The woman reacted joyfully.

"Tell her they'll be home as soon as it is safe to travel," Sam said, "and find out if she needs us to do anything for her in the meantime."

Nora conveyed the message, and then listened intently. "Frau Heidtmann wants you to know that she is fine. She thanks you very much for coming by."

"Tell her it was my pleasure. And we'll get in touch with her if we have any more news."

Nora conveyed the message. Goodbyes were said. Soon Nora and Sam were on the way again. And although they didn't have the wind blowing into their faces, it was still rough going. By the time they arrived back at the house, they were both out of breath and chilled to the bone. Sam helped Nora out of her snowshoes and into the house.

They were still shivering as they took off their coats. "We've got to get you out of these clothes and into something warm and dry," Sam said.

"You too," Nora teased, shivering.

Mindful of the others sleeping in the house, they tiptoed up to the third floor, then went their separate ways, and met up again downstairs in the kitchen. Sam used the gas-powered stove to make some hot cocoa for both of them. When it was ready, Sam put two cups, the pot of cocoa and a plate of sugar cookies on a tray. They went back into the living room. Nora settled on the sofa and poured cocoa into cups while Sam knelt to build up the fire.

"Your life as a small-town sheriff sure is interesting," Nora remarked as she sipped her cocoa. "I'm beginning to think there's never a dull moment." She studied him over the rim of her cup. "How did you end up being one?"

Sam stood. "When I was a kid, we had a family of bullies move into Clover Creek. They were big and mean and made life miserable for everyone. And the sheriff we had then didn't do anything about it. Maybe he was afraid of them, too. I don't know." Sam shook his head and retrieved a colorful hand-knit afghan draped over the back of a nearby wing chair. Coming back to her, he settled down beside her and draped the blanket over both their laps. "Anyway, eventually the townspeople got mad enough and elected a new sheriff. He came in and cleaned things up, a couple of the bullies went to jail, the others moved on, and overnight Clover Creek went back to being a great place to live again."

Sam was silent a moment, remembering the way his emotions had run the gamut from fear to disillusionment to community pride. "And that's when I knew what a difference a good law enforcement officer can make to a community," he finished solemnly.

Nora munched a sugar cookie thoughtfully. "How old were you at the time?" she asked.

Sam smiled, thinking how nice it was to be here with her like this. "I was eight."

"And you never changed your mind and wanted to do something else?"

Sam reveled in the feeling of her beside him. "Nope."

Nora sipped her cocoa and nodded curiously at his Eastern Kentucky University sweatshirt. "Did you attend EKU?"

Sam nodded. "I majored in law enforcement there. What about you?"

"I went to the University of Pennsylvania, and majored in business." Nora's mood grew reflective. "Being there put me on the fast track to success."

"Is that how you met the man you were going to marry?" Sam asked. Finishing his cocoa, he leaned forward and put the cup aside.

"No. Geoff is an old family friend. We've known each other since we were in kindergarten. But you're right, he did go to Penn, too."

Sam thought about an intimate friendship that dated back years and wondered how he could compete with that in the time frame of just a few storm-driven hours. "You must've dated a long time," he remarked.

Abruptly Nora's look turned troubled. She put her own cup aside and turned toward him. "No, never. I mean, we hung out together and did a lot of the same stuff socially, but it wasn't until a few months ago, after I got downsized out of my job in New York City and he came to cheer me up, that we started seeing each other in anything but a platonic light.''

Sam studied Nora gently. ''You didn't see the loss of your job coming?''

''No.'' Nora's lips curved wryly as she thrust both hands through her hair and recalled, with no little amount of embarrassment. ''In fact, strange as it may sound, I was doing so well at L and B, I thought I was in line for another promotion.'' She paused and bit her lip. ''I knew there'd been a couple of key accounts lost that they were unable to immediately replace, and that they were planning to downsize as a result, to sort of shake things up and light a fire under those remaining. Still,'' she continued ruefully, ''it was a rude awakening to find myself unemployed, along with about twenty others.''

Sam wished he'd been there to help her deal with the bad news, even if he had no experience with the kind of pampered Ivy League school life she'd obviously come from. ''So what'd you do?'' he asked casually, stroking her wrist.

Nora bolted to her feet and went over to prod needlessly at the fire. ''My father convinced me to take some time off and go back to Pittsburgh to recoup,'' she replied, replacing the poker in the stand. Whirling toward him, she stood with her back to the flames. ''I hadn't had any real time off in a long time, and I agreed.'' She shrugged, the movement molding her ivory cashmere sweater against the soft swell of her breasts. Color swept into her cheeks. ''Before I knew it, I was seeing a lot of Geoffrey, and then we were engaged."

He regarded her speculatively. "It must have been a very romantic time."

Nora frowned at the toe of her fleece-lined slipper. "Confusing is more like it." She sighed and shoved her balled fists into the pockets of her ivory wool trousers. "Geoff and I were both feeling a little sorry for ourselves, because we hadn't yet met the loves of our lives, and we were both tired of waiting for the mythical lightning bolt to hit us. He told me he'd begun to think passion and romance wasn't everything, that you could have a good marriage—maybe even a better marriage—without it."

Sam tossed the blanket aside and went to stand beside her. "You bought that?"

Nora flashed him a sheepish grin. "It seemed logical at the time. But maybe I was just rationalizing my mistake," she continued honestly. Looking up into his eyes, she released a beleaguered sigh. "Anyway, in retrospect, I can't help thinking it's foolish to put everything into a job and nothing into your personal life. Because if something happens with your job, you've got nothing left to sustain you."

Sam nodded, in total agreement. Wanting to comfort her, if only with a brief touch, he gently caressed the side of her face with the flat of his hand. "I want marriage and a family, too, in addition to a job I love."

"And yet you're not married," Nora murmured softly.

"Only because I'm still looking for the right

woman," Sam allowed, as he hooked his thumbs beneath her chin and tilted her face to within kissing distance of his. He lowered his mouth to hers, felt her soft gasp, felt her tense in anticipation. And still the desire in her was nothing compared to his.

"And that would be...?" Nora gasped, as he tilted her head back and kissed her temples and cheeks over and over again, until she trembled in his arms and looked up at him, all soft and wanting beneath the thick veil of her lashes.

Sam drew back slightly. "Someone who not only shares my dreams and values, but responds to me as passionately as I respond to her," Sam murmured thoughtfully as he slid a hand beneath her hair, to the back of her neck. Nora arched toward him, and Sam lost himself in the hot, wild sweetness of her lips. Giving in to the passion flowing between them every bit as readily as she had earlier in the day, Nora moaned and let her head fall back, giving him even fuller access to her mouth. Clamping an arm around her waist, Sam urged her even closer, so that they were so close their bodies were almost one. That, too, felt incredibly perfect and right. His own body aching, he continued wooing and seducing her until her body melted softly against his, until he was sure she wanted him every bit as much as he wanted her, until he was sure she knew, as did he, that what they were feeling was something special and unique.

Then, and only then, did Sam force himself to slow down.

He wanted Nora with all his heart and soul, but he didn't want to scare her off by coming on too strong, too soon. And despite her increasingly passionate response to him, he knew she was still a little skittish. And if he didn't stop now, with his desire to make love to her deepening with every second that passed, he would end up taking her to bed, before she was ready. And that, he realized, might ruin everything. As rare as what they'd found was, it would be better to wait until she was definitely ready to take the next step than to face any more regrets in either of their lives or end what looked as if it could be the love of his life.

When the leisurely kiss came to a slow, deliberate halt, Sam rested his forehead against hers while they both caught their breath.

"Sam?" Nora murmured as she rested her cheek against his shoulder.

Sam tightened his arms around her. He loved the way she felt against him. "Hmm?"

She put her hand on his chest and pushed far enough away to be able to see up into his face. "What will you do when you find this soul mate you're looking for?" Nora asked.

That was easy. Sam grinned down at Nora's searching look, and he possessively tightened his hold on Nora. "I'll marry her, the first chance I get."

Nora looked up at Sam. Had she not had a chance to get to know Sam a little, and see him in action during the course of the afternoon and evening, she might have thought he was just giving her a line to try to get her into bed with him. But she knew him well enough by now to look into his golden-brown eyes and realize he was dead serious. He did want to get married, and soon. The question was, with one disastrous near-marriage so recently behind her, what did she want? Or, more to the point, what did she dare?

She stared up at Sam, knowing her eyes reflected the mixture of wariness and desire she felt. For a moment, as the silence stretched out between them, she was unable to get her breath. "No long engagements for you, hmm?" she quipped at last.

Sam shook his head firmly. "Not if I have my way about it," he said.

He wasn't kidding. Once he'd found what he wanted—and it seemed to her that he was hinting in a million and one ways that he just had—Sam was the kind of man who would move fast, to stake his claim before the blizzard ended. Maybe too fast for an inexperienced woman like Nora. After all, wasn't this what she'd done before? Jumped into her relationship with Geoff too soon, when her life was in ruins? She didn't want to risk everything and do the same with Sam, no matter how fiercely and irrevocably she was attracted to him.

Deciding some caution was in order, for both their sakes, Nora turned away from Sam and shot a look at the grandfather clock in the corner. It was almost one o'clock. "It's getting late."

"You're right," Sam agreed lazily, although, unlike her, he seemed in no hurry for them to part company. "Morning'll be here before you know it," he said matter-of-factly as they carried their cups into the kitchen.

For a moment, their glances held. She tried, but

could not decipher what he was thinking. "I'll go up with you," Sam said.

As they walked upstairs, Nora felt the same kind of tension she usually felt at the end of a first date. But that was ridiculous, she told herself sternly. This was not a date, and Sam was not walking her to her door. And he was most definitely not going to kiss her again.

He did, however, go into her room and stoke the fire before adding another log to the hearth. Nora thanked him and ushered him to the door.

He turned at the portal and gently touched the side of her face. "Wake me if you're not warm enough or need more blankets," Sam said.

Nora knew the gallant offer was given as a matter of course, due to her previously noted inexpertness at building fires in the hearth; nevertheless, it sent a shiver of awareness rushing through her and a telltale flush to her cheeks. Ignoring the tantalizing whiff of his cologne that stirred her senses, she crossed her arms in front of her and stepped to the side. "I think I'll be fine," she told him dryly, as she focused on the new, ardent lights in his golden-brown eyes.

"Sure now?" Sam teased, studying her with growing curiosity, and making no secret of the fact that he would very much like to kiss her again.

Nora wanted to kiss him again, too. What stopped her was the knowledge that although their first kisses had been impulsive, another kiss at this point in the evening would not be. Another kiss would change the stakes between them considerably. As much as she wanted to experience the delicious feeling of Sam's lips on hers and his strong arms around her once again, she wasn't sure she was ready for their relationship to deepen. Until she was, she'd just have to make sure they both exercised a little caution. "Good night, Sam," she said.

Sam gave her a look that upped her pulse another notch. Then he smiled. "Good night."

Chapter Six

Nora woke at dawn to the rumbling noise of a snow-plow and a room that was filled with sparkling white light. Pushing off the covers, she padded barefoot to the window. Several inches of snow had fallen over-night. And for the moment, anyway, even though the sun and sky were obscured by an oppressive layer of heavy white clouds, the wind had died down, and it appeared to have stopped snowing entirely.

With no sun to warm things up, it looked bitterly cold outside, and woodsmoke curled from the chim-ney of every home on the stately tree-lined street. Nora noted that Sam was already outside. He was dressed in his uniform and shoveling the snow away from his black-and-white truck. His granddad and Kimberlee were bundled up, too, and working on the sidewalks while the snowplow cleared a path through the street.

Feeling guilty for having slept later than everyone else, Nora showered quickly, dressed and hurried downstairs. Following the aromatic scent of coffee perking and bacon frying, she headed for the kitchen. Even before she reached it, she could hear that the small transistor radio was broadcasting the weather report, and she paused a moment to listen. "...blizzard still continues to rage in many states...though many areas do not have power or have phone outages...locally, temperatures warming slightly, with more snow on the way for all of West Virginia, today and tonight. Additional possibility of sleet as the slow-moving front passes over the state. The interstate highways remain closed across the entire tristate area. Many locations in rural West Virginia are still without electricity and telephone, and crews are working around the clock to get service restored. Stay turned for more bulletins throughout the day...."

Nora continued on into the kitchen. Seeing Clara standing contentedly at the stove, an apron tied around her waist, Nora was inundated by memories of her own mother cooking her breakfast on winter mornings, and a wave of nostalgia rushed through her. What would it be like to live here all the time?

"Good morning, Nora," Clara said cheerfully.

"Good morning." Nora smiled at her. "What can I do to help?"

Clara gave the bubbling cereal a stir. "Call everyone in for breakfast. They won't want to come, the men especially, but they need to eat before they tackle the rest of their day."

Clara was right, Nora quickly noted as she executed her assigned task. The men didn't want to break and come in, but they did anyway. Short minutes later, their boots off and their faces ruddy-cheeked from the cold, they were all gathered around the breakfast table in the huge country kitchen. A fire burned warmly in the hearth, and more heat came from the big gas-powered stove. The candle-lanterns had been put out in favor of the daylight streaming through the windows.

Clara looked at Sam as he dug into his oatmeal. "Any word when the power will come back on?"

He shook his head. "The utility company crews are out looking for the downed lines now." Before he'd even finished, a radio emitted a staticky sound on his belt. "Excuse me." Sam got up and left the room. When he came back, he was already shrugging on his coat. "That was the EMS dispatcher at the fire station. There's been a two-car collision at the intersection of Oak and Main."

"Anyone hurt?"

"Yes. I've got to go." He looked at his grandparents. "I don't know when I'll be back. It looks to be a busy day."

"Stay warm and stay safe."

Sam nodded in acknowledgment and looked straight at Nora. "If you need anything," he told her softly, "don't hesitate to give me a call."

Clara's eyes danced with a romantic speculation that remained unvoiced. "At least take some coffee and a couple of rolls with you," Clara told Sam as she handed him a hastily packed paper bag and thermos.

"Thanks." Sam said goodbye and headed out the door.

"Well, I don't have to go anywhere," Kimberlee said after breakfast as they all pitched in to help clear the table.

Nora was glad to see that the teen had apparently recovered from her fight with her brother the previous evening.

"School's already been canceled," Kimberlee continued.

"Most of the businesses in town have been closed, too," Harold said.

"Including Whittakers," Clara said.

"So is it okay if I go sledding with my friends?" Kimberlee asked eagerly, after she put the last dish away and hung up her dishtowel. "I saw Ryan outside when I was shoveling snow, and he said a bunch of kids were meeting down at the park at eight this morning."

"As long as you dress warmly, and come back in time for lunch," Clara said.

"Thanks, Gran," Kimberlee said. She kissed her grandmother's cheek and dashed out.

Clara turned to Nora. "Maybe today would be a good day to ask you some advice. You did say you were in advertising, Nora?"

Nora nodded. The family had been so nice to her, she wanted to help in any way she could.

Harold led the way into the living room. "Whittakers was established by my grandfather in 1906, and it's been a family-run business ever since. We serve all the surrounding towns, as well as tourists going back and forth to the mountains."

"The problem is, we've been steadily losing business to the malls in Charleston, which are over an hour away, even though our department store has many of the exact same items offered at the mall stores, at even lower everyday prices," Clara explained unhappily as they all took a seat. "We've been thinking of hiring an advertising firm to help us pump up business. But since you have experience from the New York advertising world and are here with us, we thought we'd ask your advice first."

"Of course, we'd pay you for your time," Harold added quickly as he shot Nora a concerned glance. "We wouldn't want you to feel we're taking advantage."

"You wouldn't be taking advantage," Nora replied. "And there's no need to pay me a consulting fee. I'm happy to do this for you. Now, what advertising do you already do?" Nora asked.

"At the moment, we just run ads in the *Clover Creek Weekly*."

Clara went to get a sample to show Nora. The ad consisted of a black-and-white photo of the interior of the store, and a rather fuzzy picture of Clara and Harold and several of their employees. Unfortunately, the vast selection of quality merchandise and the charm and friendliness of the store did not come through.

Clara frowned and wrung her hands. "It's bad, isn't it?"

"It could be a little more on target," Nora offered gently. "But that's something that can be fixed pretty easily. What area of the store generates the most sales for you?"

Clara and Harold exchanged baffled looks. "I really don't know," she said. "We keep sort of a revolving inventory. We replace items as they sell. But as for which department generates the most business or which items go the most quickly..." The Whittakers exchanged looks again, and Clara finished, "We really couldn't say."

"Well—" Nora said as the electricity came back on with a snap, and they all smiled and cheered.

"Hallelujah," Harold said. "Now we really can get down to business. Please continue, Nora."

"First, we need to identify your customer base," she said as Clara walked around the kitchen to switch off the lights that were no longer needed and the television set.

"Most of that information is down at the store, along with copies of all our back advertising." Harold got up to check the phone; finding it still inoperative, he shook his head in disappointment.

Nora, however, was only relieved. As long as there were no phone lines running, there could be no faxes sent to Sam regarding her disappearance. No calls from her father. No way of easily tracking her down to Clover Creek.

"If you want to go to Whittakers with me, I can show you where everything is," Harold said. "Since the snowplow's been clearing the streets inside the city limits of Clover Creek, I think we could drive a couple of blocks."

"That'd be great, actually," Nora said.

Doing an analysis of their business problems would not only give her a chance to pay them back for their hospitality; it would also give her a chance to do her first solo job on a smaller account. That experience, plus a good reference from Harold and Clara Whittaker, would be invaluable when it came to setting up her own business.

"I hope you don't mind if I don't stay with you," Harold said an hour later, after opening his files and turning on his computer and showing Nora where all the records on sales and copies of past advertising efforts were filed. "I've got to go by the volunteer fire department and see if they need any help."

"It's no problem." Nora smiled. "It's going to take me quite a while to go through all this."

"When should I come back for you?" Harold asked.

Nora considered the analysis ahead of her. "Would it be a problem if I spent the entire morning here?" she asked. Now that the building had heat, it was comfortable and quiet.

"Not at all. I'll come back for you at noon, then," Harold said.

Nora nodded, already deeply immersed in the challenging problem in front of her.

SAM TRUDGED BACK to the sheriff's office, after a morning spent in the cold and snow. He didn't know what made people in such a hurry to get out and about in weather like this. He only knew it created nonstop problems for emergency personnel and law enforcement.

Thus far that morning, there'd been two car accidents, four stalled vehicles, a chimney fire, a cat stuck in a tree, a broken traffic light, a shattered window from an out-of-control snowball fight and a shoplifting eight-year-old at the grocery store.

Fortunately, there was some good news, too. He'd learned via police radio that the schoolteacher and seven students feared missing had telephoned their school. Something about car trouble deep in the mountains after they'd lost their way. The young mother and baby from Maryland had also been located. The mom had eloped to Kentucky, apparently flabbergasting all those who knew her.

Aware that it was only noon, he wondered what the rest of the day would hold. And that was when he saw the light on over at the store in the third-floor offices. Generally speaking, his grandparents did not even go in to the store on days when school and work were called due to weather. Adding to his suspicion, his grandfather's car was not parked out front, as it would have been if his grandparents were there.

Hoping they didn't have a visit from the burglary ring currently working the state, Sam took out his keys and headed across the street to the store. He used the employee entrance off the alley and the service elevator off the storerooms. The smell of freshly brewed coffee from the staff lounge on third had him relaxing. Maybe someone was working here.

The sight of Nora riffling casually through the files in his granddad's office had him tensing again. He hadn't been betrayed this way since he was engaged to Susan. Fool that he was, he'd been so attracted to her, he didn't expect it then. He didn't expect it now. But that didn't mean it wasn't happening, Sam warned himself sternly.

Still, Sam knew he shouldn't jump to conclusions. It was possible there was a damn good explanation for what was happening here. He only hoped Nora would give it.

"I'm surprised to see you here," Sam began, in a low, insinuating tone.

Though Sam's words were calm, there was something overly predatory and watchful in his manner that immediately set Nora's nerves on edge. She straightened, feeling her pulse skitter and jump. "I'm reviewing some back advertising for your grandparents."

To her growing consternation, Sam looked as though he did not believe her. And that, in turn, reminded Nora of all the times her father—and Geoff, too, as she had recently discovered—had lacked faith in her. She did not want to be put in a situation where her every move was questioned again.

"Mind if I check that out?" Sam asked with a highly speculative glance.

"As a matter of fact," Nora said as she crossed the room and put her hand firmly over his before he could remove the shortwave radio on his belt, "I would."

"Why?" Sam countered, just as coolly, as he removed his hand from hers and stepped back a pace. He looked down at her in a way that made her feel both trapped and accused. "If you've nothing to hide..." He shrugged and let the provoking thought trail off.

Nora tilted her head back another notch and glared up at him defiantly, determined to come out the winner in this battle of wills if it killed her. "I don't like having my every move checked up on or questioned,'' she enunciated. That was, in fact, exactly what she was running from. "It makes me feel smothered.'' *And disrespected and unappreciated.*

"Well, then, we're even,'' Sam replied as he continued to study her skeptically, "because I don't like it when my family is taken advantage of, their hospitality betrayed.''

"So who's taking advantage?'' Nora retorted, all the more bewildered and incensed by his sudden shift in attitude toward her. "I told you what I'm doing here,'' she said, making no effort to hide her mounting irritation, as she pressed a hand against her chest. "I told you I have your grandparents' permission to be looking at all of this. Even if you couldn't figure that out for yourself—'' she waved her arm dramatically "—my word on the matter should be enough!''

"And maybe it would be,'' Sam shot back, just as emotionally, "if—''

Nora waited for him to continue. When he didn't, she prodded. "What? What were you going to say?''

Sam grimaced and fell maddeningly silent. He shrugged and turned away. "Nothing.''

He was sure in a weird mood, Nora thought. Was he worried she was a spy for a rival department store, or a gifted embezzler? Heaven knew, with the right security codes, all sorts of electronic fund transfers could be arranged these days via computer. Not right now, of course, with none of the modems that would have connected them to the banks working, because the phone lines were down. But once someone had garnered that information, as soon as the lines were up again, transfers could be done at any time, from any location and any computer. Nora supposed, given all that, plus the unexpectedness of her appearance here, riffling his grandparents' private files, Sam had a right to be worried.

Then again, given the time he had spent with her, the way he had kissed her, he should trust her a little more, no matter how things looked!

Her emotions in turmoil, Nora studied Sam. She'd been around him long enough to know it wasn't like him to fly off the handle, or falsely accuse without a damn good reason. Therefore... "There's something going on here...." she theorized calmly. "Seeing me here, like this, going through your grandparents' files, triggered something in you. I'd like to know what it is."

He regarded her stoically, but made no move to illuminate her in any way. "Has it happened before?" Nora persisted doggedly, following him to the window. "Did someone steal from the store or your grandparents? Did someone betray *you* in some way?"

Sam turned away from Nora so abruptly she knew she'd struck a nerve. "Tell me," she insisted.

"I don't want to talk about this, Nora," he told her gruffly as he headed for the door.

After the curious way he'd behaved, Nora wasn't about to let him off that easily. She sprinted after him and caught his arm. Her hand on his bicep, Nora forced him to face her.

The heat and strength of the tensed muscles beneath her fingertips sent a thrill rushing through her. "Then what do you want from me, if not talk?"

"The truth?" Sam murmured, as he shook his head at her in silent remonstration.

"Yes," Nora whispered back softly, aware that her heart was pounding so hard and so fast she could hardly stand it.

Sam dragged her all the way into his arms. He tunneled his hands through her hair. "I want this."

Chapter Seven

His kiss caught her by surprise. Nora was completely unprepared for the soft, sensual feel of his lips on hers. And just as completely enthralled, as he brought her closer yet and gave her a long, thorough kiss meant to shatter her resolve. She knew she shouldn't be giving in to the desire that simmered whenever they were near each other. And yet, no one had ever made her feel this way, and she sensed that no one else ever would. So what was the harm, she wondered dizzily, returning Sam's kiss, when no one but the two of them would ever know they'd succumbed to passion? What was the harm, she thought, as another delicious shudder swept through her body, in finding out what it would be like to have a wild, passionate fling—*just once*—in her life?

Sam's kiss was both sweeter and more demanding than he intended, but try as he might, he couldn't seem to put on the brakes. He wanted Nora to feel as overwhelmed as he did by what was happening here, he wanted her to feel pushed to the absolute limit. And once that happened, he wanted to make love to Nora for a luxuriously long time. He wanted her to feel everything it was possible to feel. And then sleep wrapped in his arms, only to wake and make love again and again. But he also wanted their lovemaking to happen for all the right reasons. And right now, despite the fact that he believed with all his heart and soul, as did she, that she had never really loved her fiancé, he was not entirely convinced that was the case.

Right now, there were so many other reasons why she could be melting against him, and kissing him with such urgent need. Revenge—not to mention *consolation,* via a whirlwind storm-induced affair—being paramount among them.

Sam did not want their time together to be something Nora looked back on with regret; it meant too much to him. With effort, he forced himself to slow down and pull back from the deliciously exciting kiss. Nora shivered in his arms, but did not pull away as he wordlessly studied her upturned face and the conflicting emotions he saw in her eyes.

She wanted him desperately, but even while her body was saying yes, a small, protective part of her was still saying, No, I'm not ready for this.

"Why did you stop?" Nora whispered.

To protect you, Sam thought as he studied the wildly throbbing pulse in her throat. "Because I needed to know," he told her huskily, as he scanned her hotly from head to toe, "if you would want me so much if your wedding hadn't just been called off."

Nora's eyes widened with shock, and she stared at him in amazement. *"What?"*

Feeling they were still too close for comfort—it

was hard to think about anything but making love to Nora when they were still molded together that way—Sam dropped his hold on her. His eyes still on her face, he stepped back a pace and repeated the question.

Nora flushed. "I don't know what you're thinking, Sam Whittaker..."

He gave her a deadpan look. "Don't you?"

"...but my near miss at the altar is beside the point," she continued haughtily, tossing her head.

Sam's heart pounded in his chest as he thought about all that was at stake, the least of which was his rapidly growing feelings for her. "Is it?" he drawled, in a provoking manner meant to make her face the cold reality of the situation, whether she wanted to or not.

Nora threw up her arms in frustration. "Listen, Sam," she retorted, her pretty green eyes flashing with unbridled temper, "I'm free to do as I please here, no matter what anyone else thinks!"

Sam trod closer and gave her a know-it-all look that belied the hurt he felt inside. "What about if you were still in Pittsburgh?" he shot back smugly. "Would you be doing this there, too?"

Nora didn't answer Sam's question right away. But then, Nora realized in mounting frustration, she didn't have to answer. It was clear that Sam had already made up his mind about what was going on here, she realized sadly. Worse, he was no more prone to listen to her than her father was!

Sam sighed and shook his head in disappointment. "Just as I thought," he pronounced grimly. "You probably can't think of a better way to wreak your revenge on Geoff and your dad than by immediately getting involved with someone—anyone—else as soon as possible.''

Nora rolled her eyes. ''I readily admit the idea of hurting Geoff the way he hurt me has some appeal, but this is not the way I'd choose to do it, Sam.''

''What would your father have to say if he knew about us?''

''Oh, probably something like—'' Nora dropped her voice to a low, gruff parody of her father's serious - to - the - point - of - being - beside - himself-tone ''—'Let me get this straight, Nora. You went straight from almost marrying one man and into the arms of another?''' Nora gave Sam a level look as she continued matter-of-factly, ''He'd think it was strictly a rebound romance. And, as usual, he'd be wrong about what was going on with me.'' *She'd never felt like this. Never.*

''And yet it pleases you to know he'd be irritated?'' Sam persisted, his eyes darkening grimly.

Nora feigned a nonchalant attitude meant to irk him. ''In a perverse sort of way, sure, it pleases me,'' she admitted honestly. ''And you want to know why? Because I'm still ticked off, too!''

Sam continued to grill her. ''Is the speed with which we've become interested in each other the only thing that would bother your father about me?''

Unfortunately, Nora was no better at reading her father's mind than he was at reading hers; if she had been able to second-guess Charles Kingsley with any degree of accuracy, she would have guessed about the prenup! Nora shrugged indifferently as Sam sauntered closer. "I don't know. It's hard to say. You're certainly different from any of the men I've dated before." And, Nora thought, there was no denying that was a big part of Sam's appeal to her. The fact that Sam was so completely different from the exceedingly eligible beaux her father had thrown her way. The fact that Sam was so strong and honest and principled, and completely uninterested in her father's many connections and business holdings. The fact that he wanted to protect her enough that he would circumvent his own considerable desire, just to make sure they were doing the right thing for her, too.

"So, in other words," Sam said unhappily, "you're using me to widen the rift between you and your dad, and probably further alienate your ex-fiancé, as well, so he won't pursue you."

Nora figured her father was not likely to approve of anyone but Geoff at this point. But that was neither here nor there, as far as she was concerned. It was her life. It was her decision.

Again, Sam jumped the gun. "Dammit, Nora, I'm not in the business of separating families—rather, bringing them together!"

Nora rolled her eyes and regarded Sam with exasperation. She knew he took his job as sheriff and all-round peacemaker seriously, but he was really overstating his importance here. "You are not widening the gulf between me and my father in any way," she told him sternly. "My father and I are already oceans apart, for reasons that have absolutely nothing to do with you or anyone else. Furthermore,

I am not using you to strike back at anyone! I'm relieved and happy I didn't marry Geoff.''

Sam relaxed slightly. "I can see that," he murmured thoughtfully.

"Then...?" Nora asked.

He took her by the shoulders and held her in front of him. "I still think I've struck a nerve." Sam paused and gave her a look that seemed to go straight to her soul. "You've done it before, haven't you, Nora? Gotten involved with the wrong person, simply to irritate your father?"

Nora flushed guiltily. How did he sense these things about her? It was unnerving!

"Want to tell me about it?"

If she didn't, he would think she made a habit of this. And nothing could be farther from the truth. Ignoring the weight of his hands on her shoulders, Nora clamped her arms in front of her. "It was the year my mother died," she retorted defiantly. "I was fifteen, and I didn't do it consciously. I did it because I was scared and alone and I needed my dad and he was so wrapped up in his own grief that I couldn't get his attention any other way."

"What about the rest of your family and your friends?" Sam asked. His voice was soft, conciliatory.

Nora felt her eyes fill with tears at the memory of that difficult, lonely time. "I didn't have any other family," she said thickly. "My Mom, Dad and I were it, as far as family went, and my friends had never lost a parent, so they didn't understand what I was going through, either." She wiped her eyes with her fingertips. "So I started hanging out with a very wild crowd. They didn't care what I'd been through. Their only goal was to party like there was no tomorrow. And that worked for me, because at the time, having just lost my Mom, I didn't feel there was going to be any tomorrow." Nora released a quavering breath. "Not any tomorrow I was interested in, anyway."

Sam took her wrist in hand and led her over to the sofa. The next thing Nora knew, he was sitting down and she was on his lap. "Suffice it to say, your dad woke up to what was going on?"

Nora smoothed a hand over the front of Sam's shirt. "Not until he caught me sneaking out my bedroom window at 2:00 a.m, to meet my bad-news boyfriend. Anyway," she continued, fastening her eyes on the strong column of Sam's throat, "that's when he became smotheringly protective."

Nora sighed. "Since then, I've tried desperately to make it up to my father, so he would trust me, only that hasn't worked, either—because my dad still thinks I can't tie my own shoelaces without him."

"I see." Sam gently stroked her hair. "So now that you're in a crisis situation again, you're back to doing something you know'll upset him to make your points with him."

Nora laced her arms around his neck. She was confused about many things, but not about this. "That's not why I kissed you the way I did, Sam," she said. And she didn't want him thinking it was.

"Then why?"

Nora sucked in her breath at the unexpected gentleness in his voice, and moved back slightly, settling her weight more comfortably on his lap. "Sure you want to know?"

He nodded, every inch of him taut, demanding and ready to kiss again. "Yes."

The moment drew out as she gazed into his eyes. The compassion and willingness to understand that she saw there gave her a courage she'd never dreamed she had. For the first time in her life, she dared to proceed on a wing and a prayer. "Because I'm attracted to you in a way that I've never been to anyone before," she admitted, speaking straight from her heart, with a galvanizing honesty that she knew might change their lives forever. "And I want to explore it," she said as a self-conscious color filled her cheeks. "I want to know firsthand what all the books and movies and songs are about." More than anything, she wanted to be loved, and to love in return. If she had done that earlier—found this earlier— maybe what happened with Geoff would never have happened!

"And you think I can show you that?" Sam asked as he took her hand and gently kissed the inside of her wrist.

Nora nodded, her blood heating at the feel of his warm lips caressing her skin. "I think you're *the only one* who can show me." Wanting him to understand, she rushed on, doing her best to explain. "For as far back as I can remember, I've been so busy working and trying to prove myself that I've missed so much of the wonderful, pleasurable things in life, and now here I am, practically spinster age, with absolutely nothing to show for it on the personal side—

and…and I don't want to be that way anymore, Sam. I don't want to be a person who only has their work. I want to have something else, too." *I want to have you.*

Sam interrupted her fiercely, pulling her closer. "You're not old, Nora. And you're certainly not a spinster."

About that, they were not bound to agree. "Trust me, Sam," Nora retorted dryly, the prospect of further intimacy with Sam making her heart beat all the harder. "I know how old I am. Twenty-nine." Aware that she'd put everything she ever wanted on the line with her candor, Nora paused to draw a bolstering breath. "I don't want to reach thirty without—without having experienced one wild, crazy, madly passionate, maybe even ill-conceived love affair, no matter how long it lasts." Aware that she was tingling everywhere, she stopped and bit her lip. "I guess the bottom line is…I don't want this chance to have a wildly satisfying love affair pass me by. And I was really hoping you wouldn't, either."

Able to see that she'd caught him completely off guard with her unprecedentedly candid confession, she pressed a silencing finger to his lips. "You don't have to make a decision now," she said softly, feeling a lot better now that she was in charge of the situation and her own mounting desire, not he. Because that in turn gave her control of her life again. She released a shaky breath. "I know now is not the right time or place, but at least think about it and—and let me know. And in the meantime, I'll think about it, too," she promised softly. *If I don't change my mind between now and then, I'll know it's right.*

"Like I could do anything *but* think about it after a proposal like that," Sam said.

Nora grinned. It was fun to be on the seducing side, instead of just the object of an unsuccessful seduction. Her lips curved in a slow, tantalizing smile. "Does this mean you're actually considering my proposition?"

Sam answered her with an affable grin. "You better believe it," he retorted throatily as he tightened his hold on her and rained white-hot kisses down her neck, then lingered over the incredibly sensitive skin behind her ear. "This isn't a chance I'd want to miss, either."

"Good." Nora sighed softly. Still reveling in the pleasure of his embrace, she flattened her hands on his chest and pushed back slightly. Knowing she needed more than just a strictly physical encounter with him, if this was going to be an occasion she'd remember the rest of her life, she tilted her head up and looked deep into his eyes. "But before we let this go any further, there's something you have to do, too, Sam," she said seriously. Something very important.

"What?" Sam's expression sobered. He tightened his grip around her waist.

"I've told you about my romantic past." Nora paused as their glances meshed, letting her words sink in. "Now it's your turn to confide in me."

Chapter Eight

Sam looked both skeptical of and amused by Nora's demand. "Acting on what theory?" he asked. "That confession is good for the soul?"

What was good for the soul was connecting with someone else, feeling close to him, touching his heart. And having him touch yours back, Nora thought wistfully. But, to her disappointment, it looked as if trading confidences on the most intimate level did not come as easily to Sam as did his sensual kisses. "If someone's hurt or betrayed you, Sam, I want to know. I want to help."

He regarded her skeptically. "By making love with me?"

Nora shook her head. "By listening."

But even that, she noted with disappointment, was a leap Sam found difficult to take. Before she could say anything else, footsteps sounded in the hall. Her eyes still linked with his, Nora moved off Sam's lap and got to her feet.

Sam stood, too.

Amazed at everything that had happened in their relationship in a few short minutes, they were still staring at each other as Harold Whittaker strode in. Fresh from his stint as volunteer with emergency services, he was bundled in cold-weather gear from head to toe.

Nora turned away from Sam reluctantly. She wished Sam wasn't working. She wished they could find somewhere to hide away and talk endlessly, until she had learned everything about him. And then make love over and over until she had enough memories stored away to last her a lifetime.

"Find what you needed?" Sam's grandfather asked Nora.

"Almost." Nora went back over to the desk and began gathering computer printouts of information she had collected. "I'll need a few more hours to do an analysis, but then I should be able to sit down and talk to you and Clara and offer some preliminary advice." She smiled, slipping easily into professional-woman mode. "Would late this afternoon or early this evening be okay for that?"

Harold smiled. He looked from Nora to Sam and back again, taking in the new and different tension between them, before returning his attention to business once again. "This evening would be fine."

SAM WENT HOME with his grandfather, on the pretext of getting a quick bite of lunch before he headed back out into the fray. Nora said she'd walk back to the house after she finished her paperwork. What he really wanted was to talk to his grandparents, and with Kimberlee sledding with her friends, Nora at the store and Gus not even in town yet, there was no better time than the present.

"Why didn't anyone tell me you asked Nora to do a business analysis for the store?" Sam asked as the three of them sat down to a lunch of club sandwiches and piping hot tomato soup. He'd almost blown it with Nora when he walked in and found her going through the computer files.

"We know how guarded you are about your personal life, Sam," Clara replied as she passed the crackers. "And frankly, we didn't want you to think we were doing it simply to get Nora to stay on in Clover Creek, when nothing could be further from the truth. With her experience in the New York advertising world, her opinion as a consultant is very valuable to us. Your grandfather and I are both looking forward to any insights Nora can give us."

"I'm glad to hear that, Gran," Sam replied. "'Cause, well-meant or not, your matchmaking efforts have a way of backfiring on all of us." And he didn't want anyone or anything scaring Nora away at such a delicate stage of their relationship. And Sam had the feeling—despite Nora's unexpected proposal that they have what amounted to a blizzard-induced fling during the next few days—that she was but one step away from renewed flight.

Harold cleared his throat. "Speaking of Nora..." he said as he spooned up some soup, "I couldn't help but notice when I came into the store that there was a lot of tension between the two of you."

"You might call it that," Sam said. He'd call it pure, unadulterated passion. He still couldn't believe he had actually kissed her that way, or that she had kissed him back, or that she had been so frank about her desire to make love with him, but she had, and he was just going to have to deal with that. Just as he was going to have to deal with the fact that as soon as the interstate cleared she was probably going to leave, whether they made love or not, if for no other reason than to continue her flight from her family.

Harold studied Sam. ''Does that tension between the two of you have anything to do with Susan, or your broken engagement to her?''

Yes, Sam thought as he quickly devoured his sandwich, in an roundabout way, it did. He'd thought he was over Susan's betrayal. Obviously, he still bore some residual scars, or he wouldn't have mistrusted Nora the way he had. Thank goodness he'd come to his senses in time and realized that the two women were not the same. Susan had been a woman unwilling to change, even when her behavior hurt those she professed to love. Whereas Nora seemed a woman ready to embrace change with all her heart.

''I know you haven't been serious about a woman since Susan and you broke up.'' Clara continued probing, with uncharacteristic tenacity, as they heard the front door open and close.

Finished with her soup, she set her bowl aside. ''I hope this doesn't mean you're still carrying a torch for that Mata Hari!''

Sam bristled with irritation. He did not need to be reminded how he had misread Susan from the start.

"You know I don't discuss what happened with Susan and me with anyone," he said firmly.

"Maybe you should," Nora said as she came into the kitchen to join them. "I, for one, would like to know who she is."

"Susan is Sam's ex-fiancée," Clara supplied, with a helpfulness Sam found extremely aggravating. "Susan and Sam didn't part on very good terms."

Nora arched her brows and gave Sam a smugly knowing look that said, "So! I'm not the only one who had their marriage called off, am I?"

Sam glared at his grandparents. The last thing he had wanted to do was spend what little time he probably had with Nora discussing his failed relationship with someone else.

"Thanks a lot," he murmured sarcastically as an aside, then frowned as the radio on his belt emitted a symphony of static, followed by a loud squawk.

"Saved by the bell," Clara said dryly.

Sam flushed in a way he hadn't in years, aware that Nora was still giving him intrigued looks. Now she was more curious about Susan than ever, dammit! And he was probably going to have to leave. Figuring he'd had enough of an inquisition about his romantic life to last him for quite a while, he turned on his heel, snatched up his coat and hat and headed for the door. "I'll answer the call out in my truck. Thanks for lunch, Gran—it was great, as usual."

SAM HAD JUST FINISHED taking the call for assistance when Nora came dashing out of the house, paper bag in one hand, silver thermos in the other. He leaned across the console to open the passenger door. Looking ready for action, she scooted in and handed him the lunch sack. "Let's go," she said cheerfully.

"Since when did you become my deputy?" he asked dryly, already thrusting the gearshift into reverse.

"Since I decided it was fun to ride along."

Nora smiled over at him, looking even prettier than she had the first time he laid eyes on her, with her glossy dark hair windswept and her cheeks rosy from the cold winter air.

"And in case you're wondering, the bag contains three oatmeal cookies and an apple for your dessert, the thermos hot coffee. Gran wanted you to have some dessert, even if you couldn't stay."

"What about you?" Sam asked, concerned, even as he tried not to think how much he was going to miss Nora when—if—she did go. "You didn't have time to eat."

"There's a sandwich and some cookies and an apple in the bag for me, too, if I get hungry, which I'm not right now. So," Nora prodded, her green eyes glimmering with excitement, "where are we going?"

We. Sam liked the sound of that. It was something he could get used to a lot faster than he ever would've thought.

"Over to the high school parking lot."

"What's going on there?" Nora asked as she fastened her seat belt.

"Something dangerous, from the sound of it," Sam said grimly, as he drove down the snowbanked street. He sighed. "I just hope Kimberlee's not involved."

Unfortunately, to Sam's chagrin, Kimberlee was involved. And the activity that was going on was dangerous. A rambunctious group of young people had tied sleds to the trailer hitches of several pickup trucks. The teens were jumping on the back of the sleds while the pickup trucks zigzagged across the slippery parking lot as swiftly as their drivers dared. It was like playing crack-the-whip while being dragged by a pickup. Several times, just in the minute or two while Sam and Nora were observing, the teens riding the sleds were almost thrown off the sleds.

Swearing beneath his breath, Sam got out of the truck and headed for them. When the kids finally saw him, they all took one look at his face and knew they were in for it. Sam did not disappoint.

The lecture lasted fifteen minutes. Sam took down names, confiscated the sleds and the ropes being used to pull them, then sent everyone home. Kimberlee listened right along with everyone else, then stalked back with Sam to the truck.

Her lips set mutinously, she threw herself into the back seat. Aware that he had never been more disappointed in his kid sister, or felt like more of a total failure as a big brother and legal guardian, Sam got into the driver's seat and slammed the door.

"I want you to know you have completely embarrassed me," Kimberlee told Sam tearfully.

"And I want you to know you could have been killed," Sam shot right back, just as upset as his sister. And Nora looked equally concerned—if a lot calmer than either he or Kimberlee. "Suppose one of those sleds had slid beneath the wheels of the pickup trucks?'' he demanded, turning around to face his younger sister.

Kimberlee's face flamed. "They didn't!"

"But they could have, and then what?" Sam asked, trying his best to badger some sense into her. "Do you really think the driver could have stopped in time?"

A tense, unhappy silence vibrated in the truck as Nora looked from Sam to Kim and back again.

"Kids get killed doing stupid stunts like that every year, Kimberlee," Sam said to his younger sister hoarsely. "I don't want it happening to you. I don't want it happening to any kid in Clover Creek. You got that?"

"Yes, I've got it!" Kimberlee sobbed.

"Furthermore, you ought to know better!"

"I do!" Kimberlee shouted back, throwing up both her hands.

"Then why?" Sam demanded, shooting her a querulous glance in his rearview mirror.

Tears filled Kimberlee's eyes and rolled down her cheeks. "I don't know," she whispered.

"Neither do I," Sam muttered, upset.

But it was clear that he had failed his sister yet again, Sam realized. And for that, he had a hard time forgiving himself.

The silence remained all through the drive from the high school to the Whittaker home. Her shoulders stiff with injured pride, Kimberlee climbed out.

"Kimberlee, one more thing," Sam said, before she could escape completely.

She turned around to face him.

"You're grounded," Sam continued, doing what he knew his parents would've done in the same situation.

Kimberlee sighed. "How long?" She bit the question out, just as succinctly.

"Until further notice," Sam said.

WHEW, Nora thought, aware that she was perspiring beneath her coat. And all she'd done was witness the traumatic event.

"You might as well say it. I know you're thinking it," Sam told Nora as he reached for the thermos his grandmother had packed.

Nora slipped off her shoulder harness and turned to face him. "I understand you wanting to protect Kimberlee, Sam. And she was wrong."

Sam sighed. "Just the same, you think I was a little hard on her, don't you?"

Nora nodded solemnly. "Yes, I guess I do."

Sam poured coffee into the thermos cup and quaffed it down, black, before refilling the cup again. "I've tried my hardest to do right by her."

"I think she knows that," Nora said carefully, refusing his offer to share the coffee with a shake of her head.

"But even so, you need to put all this aside and make up with her." Because he and his sister both would be miserable until he did so.

Sam gave her a skeptical glance. "Like you've made up with your father?"

Nora's slender shoulders stiffened. "It's not the

same thing, Sam," she told him stubbornly, refusing to let him turn the subject back to her.

"It looks to me like it is," Sam returned, aggrieved, leaning toward her seriously. "In fact, to me, the situations look exactly the same."

Nora swallowed around the sudden knot of emotion in her throat. "You don't know the half of what went on with me and my dad, Sam," she whispered, looking away. Or how much all of it still hurt.

Sam put his hand on hers. "Then tell me the rest," he urged compassionately.

Nora regarded him. Knowing that he was right, that she did need to unburden herself, she began, "I told you how he neglected me after my mother died."

"Yes."

"Well, when he finally woke up, he went to the other extreme and became smotheringly protective. I was only permitted to see the people he deemed acceptable. I could only accept the invitations he thought appropriate. Maybe that would have been okay, had his interference in my life stopped there, but it didn't.

"He was so anxious for me to be happy, he wouldn't let me do anything on my own merit for fear I would fail and be unhappy again."

"Like what?" Sam asked, his hand tightening protectively on Nora's.

"Like everything," Nora replied wearily. "When he found out I wanted to go to Penn, he went behind my back and created an endowed scholarship there in my mother's name, and then used his pull to get me admitted as a student there. When I found out about it a couple of years later, when another student asked me if I was any relation to *that* Kingsley, he said he had always wanted to establish a scholarship for my mother anyway.'' Nora gestured in remembered frustration.

"Fine. I couldn't really argue about that. I wanted my mother's memory to be assured, but he admitted how it looked, and he promised me he wouldn't do anything like that again.''

"But he did?'' Sam guessed.

Nora nodded. "I told him I wanted to work in New York City after graduation, and that I'd targeted six major advertising agencies there as places to look for work. He went to the one that was number one on my list and then—without my knowledge or consent—got me a job at L and B by arranging to move his company's advertising account there.'' Nora shook her head and recounted miserably, "I can't tell you how humiliated I felt when I found out via the company rumor mill.''

Sam sighed and commiserated gently. "Your colleagues must've resented you, if they thought you had gotten your job unfairly.''

"Yes, they did.'' Nora spouted off emotionally, aware that her lower lip had started to quiver. "And furthermore, they had every right to do so!''

"What happened?''

Relieved to be finally spilling her guts to someone besides Geoff—who usually took her father's side—about all of this, Nora shook her head. "I was tempted to leave, but I didn't want to let my father take that from me, too, so I dug in my heels and stayed, and toiled night and day until I had proved myself worthy of the job I had secured.'' She raked her hand through her hair, pushing it off her face. ''And I kept right on proving it long after I had decided the world of high-stakes advertising and sixty-hour workweeks weren't really for me. Meanwhile, my dream of home, family, children, seemed farther and farther out of reach.''

''Did your father sense your dissatisfaction with your life?''

''Of course.'' Feeling she had to move or she'd die, Nora pushed away from the truck.

Sam circled around to join her on the snow-covered sidewalk. ''What did he say about it?''

Nora pulled her mittens out of her pockets and inched them on. ''He wanted me to come home to Pittsburgh and work with him in the family business.''

''But you refused,'' Sam guessed.

Nora picked up a handful of snow and patted it into a ball. ''Right up until I got downsized out of my job at the advertising agency. That came as such a shock to me, even though I wasn't the only up-and-coming young exec who got the ax, that I finally did go home.''

''And then what happened?''

''What I had feared all along. My father insinuated himself in my life again, big-time. Of course, everything was done behind my back,'' Nora said as she took aim at a nearby tree, hurled the snowball and watched it splatter into a thousand tiny flakes. She whirled to face Sam. ''But when I found out how far he would still go to ensure my well-being, I knew I had to get out of there before I drowned in his good intentions.''

''That's why you left?'' Sam regarded her speculatively. ''Because your dad tried to help you and make you happy?''

Nora flushed with embarrassment, thinking about the dowry that had been paid for her hand in marriage. She still couldn't believe her father had thought he had to *buy* her a husband! Like she wasn't pretty enough or smart enough or successful enough to find one on her own! Like she couldn't have married Geoff without his help! ''Among other reasons, yes. It's also why I'm not going back,'' Nora replied stubbornly, knowing she had not made a mistake in leaving the way she had.

Sam studied her. ''There must be more to it than that,'' he said finally.

Nora picked up another handful of snow and gazed at the low gray clouds that blanketed the area as far as the eye could see.

''There probably was, knowing my dad,'' Nora returned lightly. She shuddered to think what other well-intentioned scheming might have gone on behind her back. ''But that's not the issue right now, Sam.'' Nora tossed off another snowball, with pleasing accuracy. ''What I want to talk about right now is you and Kimberlee and the continuing dissension between you.''

He interrupted her in frustration. ''I'm trying—''

Nora gently touched his arm. ''I know you are, Sam. But it's not enough just to try with a young girl her age. You need to find a way to work things out with her and get close to her again. Otherwise, she's probably going to turn more and more to her boy-friend, Kenny, and that could be disastrous. Because you're right—she probably is too young to be so wrapped up in him. So think about what I've said, Sam.''

Sam tipped his head down to hers and met her be-seeching gaze with a tender one of his own. "I will," he said, the angst draining out of him as swiftly as it had appeared. ''And you do the same.'' He touched the tip of her nose affectionately. ''Because you need to make peace with your family, too.''

Nora knew Sam was right. She just didn't know how or when, and until she figured out a way to get through to her father once and for all, she wasn't go-ing to do anything but try to repay the hospitality of the family who had so kindly taken her in during the storm that had paralyzed the entire East Coast of the United States.

So, while Sam went back to work keeping the streets of Clover Creek safe, she rolled up her sleeves and finished her analysis of the Whittakers Clothing and Department Store's advertising, and came up with a list of ways to improve it.

''I noticed from the list of charge accounts that you have customers as far as fifty, sixty miles away from Clover Creek. In fact, some of your best customers come from Peach Creek, Maplewood and Madison,'' Nora said as she sat down with the Whittakers to go over her findings.

It was late afternoon, and the temperature remained

just above freezing. The latest weather report predicted another foot of snow or snow mixed with sleet that evening, but for the moment, there was no further precipitation. Just cloudy gray skies and a feeling of foreboding that hung in the brisk winter air.

Clara smiled with pride at Nora's observation. "Some of our customers' families have had accounts that go back to the store's opening in 1906. And that's not surprising, given that we've always tried to provide the absolute best service we could. For instance, I know Sue Ellen Pritchard, over in Accoville, simply adores Liz Claiborne, so whenever we get a new shipment in I give her a call first thing."

"Whereas Jeremy Walker in Big Falls only likes Levi's brand jeans, and he and his four growing boys go through them like crazy," Harold added. "So I always make sure I have some on hand in their sizes."

"Well, then, that might be the new focus of your advertising," Nora said, as she paused to scribble a few notes on the yellow legal pad in front of her. "Not only does Whittakers have all the brands that people have come to know and love, but also specializes in highly personalized service." Noting her idea had struck a positive chord with the Whittakers, Nora continued matter-of-factly, "I noticed you don't have a catchy motto in any of your ads. You might want to commission a public relations firm to come up with one that people will remember. In addition, I think you might want to up your advertising budget considerably for the small newspapers that serve the outlying towns, where you already have some customers and could build up a lot more, if they knew you were around. And then you could also add some radio advertising...with a catchy new jingle. And consider a getting-to-know-you type sale...where you send out flyers advertising twenty-five percent off any one item in the store, the idea being to get them in the store to see what you have. I think if customers see how much merchandise you carry on a regular basis, and experience firsthand how friendly and per-sonalized the service at the store is, if they know you have much of the same merchandise they have in the malls in Charleston, only you're a heck of a lot closer, then they'll want to come back.''

''Won't all this cost a lot of money?'' Harold said, frowning.

Nora nodded. This was the difficult part of every negotiation. ''It'll cost some,'' she agreed, ''but once the initial outlay is made and everything is in place, I think you'll reap the rewards of an expanded cus-tomer base. It's up to you, of course, how much or how little you want to do.'' She sat back in her chair. ''I just urge you both to think about it.''

Clara and Harold exchanged a look.

''We'll talk it over and let you know in a day or two what we decide,'' Harold said.

Nora smiled, the satisfaction of a job well done flowing through her. She knew she had given Clara and Harold a lot to think about. ''That'll be fine.''

''SAM SHOULD HAVE been home by now,'' Clara fret-ted several hours later, looking out the window. It was 7:00 p.m., and the table was set. A hearty beef stew was simmering on the stove, a pan of homemade biscuits was ready to be slid into the oven to bake. Kimberlee was upstairs, sulking with all her might. And a light, powdery snow was coming down, coating the just-cleaned town streets and sidewalks with a thin new layer of white.

"He's probably just finishing some paperwork," Harold said soothingly, adding another log to the fire.

"You're probably right. But with the majority of the minor roads outside of town still completely snowed over, it's a worry. Especially if he's responding to a call for help on one of them."

Nora didn't want to think about Sam being in jeopardy. And since his parents had lost their lives in a car accident in inclement weather, it was easy to understand why Clara and Harold were worried. "Why not use the shortwave radio to call Sam and see if he's okay?" Nora asked, wanting to do something to take away their worry.

Clara continued pacing back and forth in front of the windows. "Sam doesn't like us using the radio for personal reasons unless it's an emergency. This would *not* constitute an emergency in his view."

"I could walk over to the sheriff's office and check on him that way," Nora volunteered with a smile. "I was thinking about taking a walk anyway."

"You're sure?" Harold asked, sliding his glasses down his nose.

"Positive. It's not far, and it's such a pretty night." Almost romantic. Plus, it'd give her a chance to clear her head, to brace herself for her next meeting with Sam. They hadn't seen each other since their discussion about Kimberlee and she wanted to be with him again.

"All right," Clara conceded.

"But if he's not there," Harold cautioned protectively, "you call us on the shortwave and I'll come and get you."

Nora bundled up and set off, noting once again how pretty Clover Creek looked, with its well-tended homes and streetlights shedding pools of warm yellow light on the banks of pristine white snow. Smoke curled from nearly every chimney she passed and scented the air with a homey wood fragrance. There was a safe, almost bucolic atmosphere on the snow-covered streets, even after dark.

Nora understood why Clara and Harold had never wanted to leave, and why Sam had come back. The small rural town was a great place to raise a family, Nora thought as she headed for the sheriff's office. Maybe one day Kimberlee would realize that, too.

When Nora approached the sheriff's office, the lights were on, the door was unlocked, but once again, Sam was nowhere in sight. "Sam?" Nora called out.

When she got no response, Nora strode to the back of the building, past the bathrooms and the lone jail cell to the soda machine by the rear door. There was still no sign of anyone.

Nora returned to the front room and started for the shortwave radio, intending to call the Whittakers. Before she could set the channel to the frequency where they'd told her they could be reached, the shortwave radio box squawked. "Clover Creek sheriff, are you there?"

Figuring someone should answer what might possibly be a call for help, Nora sat down in front of the microphone and pressed the button that would allow her to reply. "This is the sheriff's office in Clover Creek," she said authoritatively, figuring that if it was urgent, she could always get ahold of Sam or someone else on the regular police radio frequency. She leaned closer to the microphone. "How may we help you?"

"This is the Bedford City, West Virginia, sheriff's office. We've got a private investigator here from Round the Clock Investigations, looking for a runaway bride, Elanora Hart-Kingsley. We were wondering if you'd seen her."

Chapter Nine

Talk about being in the right place at the right time! "I don't know," Nora said, deadpan. "Could you describe her and tell us what she's done?" *Besides take charge of the rest of her life?*

"Well, we sent a fax of her before the storm hit. The missing woman's name is Elanora Hart-Kingsley—"

"Right," Nora said authoritatively, distressed to find the search for her picking up. "We got it." *And I destroyed it.*

"Have you seen her?"

Well, that depends, Nora thought, *on how often I look in the mirror.*

Knowing some answer was needed in reply, she said finally, "No, but I'm on the lookout for anything or anyone suspicious." Curious as to what her father and Geoff were telling people, she said, "Can you explain a little more about this woman and how she happens to be missing?"

"According to her family and the private investigator we've got here, she is brokenhearted and confused...."

Now that, thought Nora, enraged, was absolutely not true. She might be hurt, but she knew exactly what she was doing, and why!

"In addition," the Bedford City law officer said, "there seems to have been a bit of a family misunderstanding that prompted the young woman's flight."

That was an understatement and a half, Nora thought, incensed.

"Her father and her fiancé would like to find her and straighten things out."

Nora glanced out the window and saw that the snow was picking up a little, as was the wind. "What have you done in terms of the search so far?" Nora asked coolly.

"Well, before the storm hit, we sent out wedding photos of Miss Kingsley to every law office in the state. We'll be doing it again as soon as phone service is restored across the state."

Nora struggled not to groan out loud. She kneaded the tense muscles in her neck. "Do you know when that will be?"

"Soon, we hope, but right now most of the rural areas are still without service."

Thank heaven for small miracles, Nora thought, glad to have at least some good news.

"In the meantime, we're concentrating our search in West Virginia," the officer continued.

Uh-oh, Nora thought, as prickles of alarm slid down her spine. "What makes you think Miss Kingsley's in West Virginia?" she asked, as innocently as possible.

There was some shuffling on the other end, and then the private investigator from Round The Clock Investigations got on the receiver. After he introduced himself, he went back to Nora's question. "We've had reports from truckers. We put out flyers at all the truck stops before the storm hit. With people stranded, there isn't much else to talk about, and a bride driving around in a wedding dress is a sight you don't usually see."

Tell me about it, Nora thought, recalling how mortified she'd been to discover she was stuck in her wedding dress—at least until the nimble-fingered Sam helped her out of it! "What about the state highway patrol?" Nora asked cautiously, doing her best to hide her frustration. "Have you notified them?" She needed to know what she was up against.

"Yes, ma'am. Miss Kingsley's father has called literally everyone he can think of."

Damn, Nora thought. *And I thought I had a chance at remaining incognito for at least a week!*

"He's a powerful man, you know, with business interests all over the country. Anyway, you'll let us know if you see her?"

"We'll call you as soon as we have something to tell you," Nora promised sagely. *Which will be never.*

The private investigator and the sheriff's deputy both thanked her and then signed off. Finished, Nora cut the radio with a shaking hand. Dammit all, she should have known her father would not change his smothering ways. He probably still wanted her to marry Geoff!

She was really starting to like Clover Creek. And

the Whittakers. And she really, really wanted to have a whirlwind love affair with Sam. But suddenly none of that mattered. With the detectives her father had hired closing in on her, she was going to have to stick with her original plan and get as far away as possible as soon as the storm broke.

SAM WALKED INTO THE OFFICE just as Nora pushed away from the table that held the shortwave radio. "What are you doing?" Sam asked as he shrugged out his coat and hung it on the hook by the door.

Nora whirled to face him, her expression far too nonchalant to be believed. She swallowed nervously. "I was trying to radio your grandparents to tell them you weren't here."

Sam paused. He didn't need a degree in criminal justice to know something was amiss here. "Trying to or did?" Sam asked, a lot more casually than he felt. Nora was not pulling something over on him. It was Susan who had betrayed him by going behind his back.

Nora blinked up at him, looking jittery and ill at ease. "What?"

"As I walked by the window, I thought I heard the shortwave radio going," Sam repeated impatiently.

Nora looked as if she'd been struck by a bolt of lightning, and her glance shifted to the radio he carried on his belt. Her mouth opened in a round O of surprise. Her face paling, she looked up at him, "Did you hear it go off, too?"

"No," Sam replied. "I didn't." What was going on with her? Was she afraid to be alone with him, after the conversation they'd had this afternoon about the possibility of the two of them making love sometime soon? Had she had a change of heart and was afraid to tell him? Or was she still thinking along the same lines and nervous about the idea of making love?

Noting she still looked confused, Sam continued explaining, "The radio in the office is kept on a different frequency than the portable units we use. Since we're such a small operation, doing that saves a lot of confusion and keeps the portable units open for emergency use, the one here in the office available for more pedestrian matters. When the phone lines are up and running, we sometimes put the radio units all on one frequency, and use the phone for the routine stuff. Sort of depends on how much is going on. Obviously, today there's a lot going on, so we keep as many frequencies as possible monitored, so people can get ahold of us. We make the judgment on a day-by-day basis."

"So tonight the one in the office—?"

"Is only being monitored here," Sam verified. "Though it seems my deputy is out on a call."

"Oh." To Sam's consternation, Nora practically sagged with relief.

Which blew his theory that she was worried, on a romantic basis, about being alone with him. His jaw tautening, Sam advanced on Nora. "Back to my question, were you talking on the radio just now?" And if so, why don't you want to tell me about whatever it was that was said?

"Oh, that." Nora flushed and waved an idle hand

as she accidentally bumped into the edge of a desk. "I don't know much about how these shortwave radios work, and as I was trying to figure out how to call your grandparents' home, I accidentally picked up a transmission meant for someone else. It took me a moment to shut it off."

Sam studied her bluntly, his gut instinct telling him that was only a select portion of the truth. Curious as to what she was going to come up with next, Sam folded his arms in front of him. "So who was it?"

Nora tossed her hair and adopted an air that was even more girlishly innocent. "Who was what?"

Sam closed the distance between them. "That you overheard," he explained.

"Uh, I don't know." Nora zipped by him in a drift of floral perfume. Appearing distracted, she busied herself collecting her coat, mittens and hat. "I didn't hear enough to really be able to tell," she finished nonchalantly.

Sam tipped his head to the side and studied her relentlessly. He knew in his heart that Nora was no criminal. That didn't mean she wasn't up to something. And it didn't mean that she didn't need his help—because right now he had the feeling she did, in the worst way.

He stepped forward and wordlessly took her coat, mittens, and hat from her and set them on his desk. He slid his hands behind her and overlapped them, then drew her against him. "It sounded like you were talking, too," he said.

"Probably," Nora conceded in a soft, matter-of-fact voice as she splayed her hands across his chest and ducked her head, ignoring the questions in his eyes. "Whenever I get frustrated with my inability to do something, I try and talk myself through it."

Sam could believe that. She'd demonstrated from the very first second he laid eyes on her that she was a very headstrong woman. Just as she was demonstrating now, by the way she was melting against him, that there was more than unanswered questions between them. There was also a sizzling, uncontrollable desire that was not likely to ever go away. And, Sam thought on a wave of distinctly male satisfaction as their glances met and Nora drew in a trembling breath, she knew it, too.

"And speaking of frustration, have you given some thought to what we talked about earlier?"

"Yes, I want to make love to you," Sam said gruffly, knowing that was one fact not likely to change, no matter what the future heralded.

Nora flushed and rolled her eyes. "Not that. The other," she insisted softly, stepping out of the circle of his arms.

Now it was Sam's turn to be confused. "What other?" he demanded.

She answered him in one word. "Susan."

Sam loosened his tie, as if it were choking him, keeping his eyes on her face all the while. Not sure whether to resent or respect her persistence about discovering the most intimate details of his life before they did what they both wanted to do—and made love—he asked mildly, "You're really not going to let go of that, are you?"

Nora shot him a wickedly feminine smile and,

clearing a swath of papers with her hand, perched on the edge of his desk. "Not as long as it holds the key to understanding your heart."

Sam thrust his hands in his pockets and leaned back against a nearby wall, his legs crossed at the ankles, his body at a comfortable slant. While he could have done without some of her persistent questions, it pleased him that she not only wanted to make love with him—without matrimonial guarantees of any kind—but wanted to really understand him, too. "You really think it does?" he asked softly.

Nora smiled with a sweet sexiness all her own and held his eyes. "Don't you?" she retorted softly.

Sam realized that, as reluctant as he was to discuss his failed romance, he didn't want any secrets between him and Nora. Not about anything. And maybe the way to get her to confide more in him was to confide more in her first. Certainly, it was worth a try. "What do you want to know?" he asked casually, as she strolled across the room and stood next to him.

Nora leaned a slender shoulder against the wall and slanted her head back beneath his. "Everything," she said softly. "How you met her, why you fell in love with her, what happened to break it off."

"Susan was a TV reporter for the local news in Chicago," Sam said, pushing his fingers through the tousled layers of his golden-brown hair. "We met while she was doing a story."

"Was it love at first sight?"

"I don't know." Sam shrugged. "Can you love someone without really knowing them?" That was a question the two of them needed to answer, too.

Nora swallowed. "Nevertheless, you were going to marry her."

Sam nodded without remorse. "And I probably would've, had I not caught her going through the files on my laptop computer late one night when she thought I was asleep."

"What was she looking for?"

Sam sighed. Pushing away from the wall, he began to pace the office wearily. "Leads on potential stories for the TV station where she worked." Worse than his anger had been the betrayal he'd felt.

"What did she say when you caught her?"

Sam shrugged and turned his gaze back to Nora. "Pretty much what you would expect someone to say in that situation. That she was sorry. That her ambition had gotten the better of her."

"And yet you couldn't forgive her," Nora guessed, her green eyes narrowing.

"Actually, I probably could've," Sam allowed, "if she'd promised me she would never do it again."

"But she didn't," Nora said sorrowfully.

Sam shook his head, recalling without wanting to how hurt and disillusioned he had been. "Susan expected me to understand that the extraordinarily successful journalists always did whatever they had to do to get a story. And that she was one who always, always, went the extra mile in the course of her work." *Even if that meant destroying her relationship with me in the process,* Sam thought.

"And she said that, even though she knew how much she'd hurt you?" Nora looked both shocked and incensed.

Sam nodded. "And it was her stubborn refusal to change, even in the face of the realization that her actions had damn near destroyed our relationship, that made me realize she wasn't the woman I had thought—hoped—she was." He shrugged again, knowing he'd had no other choice. "And so I broke it off."

Nora studied Sam. In his own way, he was just as stubborn and single-minded as her father. The difference was, Sam was much more inclined to let her do things her own way. That meant a lot to her. More than she could have said. Because she didn't think she could get involved with someone who would go behind her back to manipulate her again—even if he thought, as first her father and now Geoff had, that it was for her own good.

Before she could comment further, the phone rang. It took a moment for it to register what a wondrous sound that was—after nearly twenty-four hours of doing without. Realizing service had been restored, Nora and Sam looked at each other. "Well, what do you know? Civilization is returning." Sam grinned as he reached for the receiver.

"Hi, Gran." He listened a moment. "That's good news. Hang on a second and let me tell Nora." He covered the receiver with his hand. "Gus just called. He's in Indianapolis."

Nora blinked and tried not to let herself think how the just-restored phone service could swiftly ruin everything about her stay in Clover Creek. Working to keep her anxiety in check—the last thing she wanted was her father's detectives catching up with her now!—she inquired casually, with a smile she knew did not quite reach her eyes, "What's Gus doing there?"

"It was the only flight he could get out of New York City last night before the storm hit and they closed all the airports. He told Gran he figured he'd go west of the storm and then head back to us that way, as the roads cleared. So far he's made it as far as Indianapolis. Even though they weren't hit nearly as hard as us over there—I think they only got about seven inches of snow and no sleet in Indiana—it's still pretty slow going. What, Gran?" Sam paused. "Gran says Gus still hopes to be here tomorrow, but Gran thinks he's being overly optimistic." Sam listened again, frowning. "Now, Gran, there's no need to panic just yet. Yes, I promise, I'll bring Nora home with me when I come, but it won't be for a while yet. I've got to stay here in case there are any more calls before things shut down for the night. Right. See you later." Sam hung up and looked at Nora. "Gran also wanted us to know a new wave of snow and sleet has already hit the West Virginia mountains south of us and is officially bearing down on us. The Weather Channel says it will hit us in about two hours. It's supposed to go on much of the night."

Nora made a face. "On top of all this snow?"

Sam nodded. "It's going to be a mess."

But it will also keep me stuck here, and protected from outside interference in my life, a little while longer.

Oblivious to her thoughts, Sam continued, "In light of that, Gran said they've gone ahead and canceled the EMS fund-raiser, due to the continued bad weather. They're going to reschedule it in a couple of weeks, rather than risk a low turnout.''

''Sounds smart.''

''Yeah, although that doesn't help the community much. We really need another ambulance as soon as possible. The people here are going to be disappointed. They'd do just about anything to get one, and I don't blame them.'' The phone rang again. ''Excuse me,'' Sam said. ''Sheriff's office.'' Then he listened intently. ''Slow down, honey. Slow down and tell me what happened. All right. Tell your dad to hold on. I'll be right there.''

''What's happening?'' Nora said.

Sam frowned. ''That was Doc Ellen's five-year-old daughter, Katie. She said Joe—her dad—fell off the ladder and has a big ouchie on his face that's bleeding.''

Oh, dear. ''Where's Doc Ellen?'' Nora asked urgently.

''Apparently she's on a house call on one of the farms outside Clover Creek. Katie said her Mom will be back soon, but in the meantime, I've got to try and get some EMS out there to help Joe.'' Sam picked up the phone and punched in a number. He listened, then identified himself and briefly explained. He paused, then swore tersely beneath his breath. ''No, no, I'll manage somehow. Thanks.''

''What is it?'' Nora asked as soon as Sam hung up, knowing that whatever it was, it wasn't good.

Sam tossed Nora her coat and grabbed his. ''Our

only ambulance is already out on a call. You and I are going to have to handle this."

"HURRY, HURRY," Katie, Ellen Maxwell's five-year-old daughter said when Sam and Nora arrived at Doc Ellen's farmhouse. "My daddy's inside and he's bleeding!"

Sam and Nora rushed past the ladder sprawled in the snow beside the front porch and into the house. Joe Maxwell was seated at the kitchen table, a snow shovel on the floor beside him. He was holding a cloth to his forehead, and he looked disoriented.

Their daughter had antiseptic and Band-Aids on the table. She climbed on a chair and posed her folded hands in front of her in a most serious manner. "Daddy won't let me touch his ouchie," she told them gravely.

"That's okay." Sam reassured the little girl with a smile. "We're here now, and we can help out. But you can watch us if you want."

"Okay." Katie scooted backward until her spine was touching the ladder back of the chair and her legs were straight out in front of her. "Mommy's going to be mad," she said with wide-eyed candor. "Mommy told Daddy not to get on that ladder if she wasn't here."

"Doesn't sound like bad advice," Sam drawled as he took the cloth from Joe's forehead and examined the gaping three-inch cut near the hairline. "What were you doing, anyway?" he asked.

Joe moaned softly—whether in remembrance of his

foolhardy actions or in response to the slight touch to his head, Nora could not tell.

"I heard there was more snow mixed with sleet on the way, and I was afraid the porch roof was going to collapse under all that weight," Joe confided miserably. "So I got the ladder out and started clearing off what I could reach with the shovel." Joe shrugged—and grimaced, as if in pain, again. "The next thing I know, my feet are flying out from under me. I think I conked my head on the edge of the gutter on the way down."

"That's what it looks like, all right," Sam said.

Joe peered up at them both. "Do I need stitches?"

Sam and Nora both nodded. "It would appear so," Nora said.

Joe groaned. "Katie's right. Ellen *is* going to kill me for this."

Sam and Nora exchanged looks. Sam held up two fingers in front of Joe's face while his daughter Katie watched gravely from her chair. "How many fingers am I holding up?" Sam asked.

"Two," Joe and Katie said in unison.

Everyone chuckled at the five-year-old's enthusiastic reply. "Well, that's a good sign," Sam drawled, winking at little Katie, "that you and your daddy are seeing the same thing."

"Maybe we should clean this out a little, while we're waiting for Ellen," Nora said, opening the first aid kit. She shot Sam a look of quiet confidence. "In fact, I can do it, if you want. I was a lifeguard for several summers during college."

"That'd be great, thanks." Sam looked at Katie,

who was still sitting patiently on her chair, but beginning to look worried again as she viewed the gaping wound. He held out his hands, and she stood and went willingly into his arms. "While Nora works on your daddy's ouchie, what do you say you and I give your mommy a call and see how much longer before she gets home?"

"WE'VE GOT to get another ambulance, Sam," Doc Ellen said an hour later, after she had stitched up her husband.

"I know." Sam patted the pacing physician's shoulder.

Ellen teared up. "If this had been even a tad more serious, I shudder to think—"

"I know," Sam reassured her firmly. "And we'll get one soon. I promise. No matter what we have to do."

Relaxing slightly, Ellen nodded. She dabbed at her eyes with a tissue and looked at Nora. "Thanks for helping. You did a good job until I was able to get here."

Nora smiled. "I was glad to be of service." In fact, it had felt good to help out. They didn't have this kind of neighborliness and camaraderie back in the neighborhood she'd lived in Pittsburgh, growing up. Not in her New York apartment building, either. In both places, it had been every man for himself.

As conversation dwindled, Nora became aware of a soft, whispery sound on the roof. It was louder than rain, softer than hail. She looked at Sam; he looked back at her. "Is that sleet?" she asked, half-afraid she already knew the answer.

"Sure sounds like it," Sam agreed as he and Nora stepped out onto the porch. Nora looked at the mixture of ice and snow raining down from the sky and groaned. Of all forms of precipitation, sleet and ice were the most dangerous.

Sam grimaced at the change in the weather and went back in to grab their coats. "We better get going," he told her, and Nora agreed. Reassured that Doc Ellen's husband was in good hands, they said their goodbyes and took off.

Unfortunately for them, a thin layer of sleet had already accumulated on top of the snow packed down on the road. It made for a treacherous combination. Sam's truck slipped and slid all over the road, losing traction as often as it gained it. "I don't think we're going to be able to make it all the way back into town tonight," Sam said grimly as he struggled to keep the vehicle on the road.

"I was thinking the same thing," Nora said, already holding on for dear life. They were only going about five miles an hour, and she was already terrified. Plus, with the mixture of sleet and snow coming down harder with every second that passed, making visibility next to nothing, it only looked to get worse.

"My place is on the next road over, and it's a lot closer than town," Sam told her. "Looks like we're going to have to bunk there for the night." He paused while her heart skipped a beat. "Is that okay with you?"

"Sure," Nora said. They were both adults. They

could handle it. And besides, wasn't this what she had wanted—an excuse to spend some uninterrupted time alone with Sam? Wasn't this what they had both wanted?

UNLIKE the frame farmhouses and log cabins owned by his neighbors, Sam's home was a modern A-frame set off the road. Sam hadn't been there since the blizzard first hit the area, and neither the sidewalk leading up to the front porch nor the driveway had been cleared. Consequently, the porch was surrounded by two- and three-foot drifts of snow. By the time they waded through the driving sleet and drifts of snow to the front door, their clothes were soaked through.

"Come upstairs with me and I'll find you something to change into," Sam said, shivering as hard as Nora as he shucked off his snow-covered boots and went around turning on lights. "After that, I've got to check in with my deputies and telephone my grandparents to let them know where we are." Sam helped Nora off with her boots and coat and placed both near the front door to dry. "Then we can see about rustling up some dinner." He turned up the thermostat and went over to start a fire in the huge freestanding flagstone fireplace that warmed both kitchen and living areas, and acted as the dividing wall between the two rooms. Satisfied the fire was going, he stood and faced her, "I take it you haven't eaten yet, either?"

Nora rubbed her hands together. "No."

"Well, don't worry," he said, taking her elbow and leading her up the stairs to the loft that contained the master bedroom and bath. "I'll see you're well taken care of."

Nora's throat went dry as she looked at the mussed covers on his king-size bed and the adjoining bath, with a glassed-in shower stall big enough for two. Oblivious to the second thoughts she was having— "Be careful what you wish for, it just might come true!"—Sam disappeared into a walk-in closet and brought out a pair of sweatpants with a drawstring waist, a matching sweatshirt and a thick pair of socks. "These are probably all way too big."

Nora shrugged. "They're warm and dry, and that's all that matters. Thanks."

While he changed in the bedroom, she changed in the bathroom and ran a brush through her hair.

Nora looked at herself in the mirror. Her cheeks were rosy from the cold and exertion. His bathroom carried the faint scent of his aftershave. There was an unsettling intimacy in being here alone with him like this. Too much intimacy, Nora thought, for two people who had not yet made love, but had—foolishly?—agreed to think about doing so.

Aware that her cheeks were pinkening even more at the thought of what might happen in the hours ahead, she turned out the bathroom light and went back into the bedroom.

She knew Sam. Nothing was going to happen that she did not absolutely want to happen.

The problem was, she knew what she wanted to happen.

Was she ready?

Only time would tell.

In the meantime, able to tell by the sound of his voice that he was already downstairs, checking in via telephone, Nora drew a bolstering breath and prepared to go down to join him.

"I DON'T HAVE A CLUE what you're talking about," Sam told his deputy.

"I just got a call from a man from Pennsylvania. We're supposed to have gotten a fax about his daughter yesterday afternoon..."

Sam froze. *Nora had burned a fax in the fireplace.*

"...and there was a shortwave radio conversation with a woman in our office earlier today."

Another wave of uneasiness washed over Sam.

Despite what she claimed, *Nora had been talking on the shortwave radio, too.*

"'Course, I wanted to know what woman in our office," Sam's deputy continued, bewildered, "since we don't have a woman working in our office at the moment, but the detective that called couldn't give me a name. I do, however, have the family's number, if you want to call."

"Yes," Sam said, waving Nora on through to the kitchen, where a fresh pot of coffee was brewing, "I do."

"EVERYTHING OKAY?" Nora asked Sam when he joined her in the kitchen fifteen minutes later. "You look kind of grim." She knew he'd been talking to his deputy—and someone else.

Sam approached her cautiously, a muscle working

in his jaw. "That's because I feel grim," he told her mildly.

Nora hitched in a breath. She did not like that look in his eyes—like he'd just found out he'd been double-crossed and was preparing to do battle. "Do I want to know why?" she asked weakly.

"Oh, probably," Sam said in a cavalier voice. He strode closer, not stopping until he towered over her. He folded his arms in front of him. "I just had a most interesting conversation with the owner of the Hamburger Heaven restaurant chain." Sam pinned her to the spot with a deadpan look. "Perhaps you know him?"

Nora's heart pounded in her chest. She should have known her father would catch up with her sooner rather than later, storm or no storm! Darn it all, anyway, it was all she could do not to turn tail and run. "What did you tell him?" she asked Sam anxiously.

Sam narrowed his eyes at her grimly. "Exactly what you'd expect a sheriff to say to a parent of a missing person—that I would do everything possible to help him find his daughter."

Chapter Ten

"You can't do that!" Nora said.

"You're right," Sam replied as he lounged against the kitchen counter and watched her put together a quick meal of bread, fruit and cheese. "*You* should do that."

Nora regarded Sam in obvious irritation. "Why?"

Sam stiffened at the accusatory edge in her voice. Obviously, she was ticked off at him for discovering what she had tried so hard to hide. He remained where he was with effort, aware that she had never looked more beautiful, with her dark hair all tousled, her cheeks flushed with anger and indignation, her lips enticingly soft and bare. "Because your dad's going out of his mind with worry, that's why," Sam explained patiently.

Nora lifted her slender shoulders in an elegant shrug. "After the way he sold me off like a piece of property, my father deserves to worry."

Sam regarded Nora, bemused. "Sold you—in this day and age?" What the hell was she talking about? Nora was as free to come and go as she pleased as any woman he had ever seen.

"I know." Nora folded her arms in front of her and leaned against the opposite counter. "I thought dowries went out of style a long time ago, too. Apparently not in my family."

Sam paused. His gut told him there was more to this. "Maybe it wasn't the way it looked," he said gently.

Nora tossed her head and fixed him with a mutinous look that let him know in a flash that her hurt was not unfounded. "My father had a prenuptial agreement drawn up between—are you ready for this?—not me and Geoff, but my father and Geoff!" Her soft lips pursed tightly, and her emerald-green eyes shimmered with fury. "He gave Geoff shares in the family business. And then, to add insult to injury, both of them went to very great lengths to keep their little arrangement from me. So, Mr.-I-Have-All-the-Answers, what would you call that?"

On the surface? A betrayal that went straight to the heart and had damn near destroyed Nora in the process, Sam thought protectively. Yet, wary of jumping to conclusions about Geoff and her father in the same way that Nora had, Sam forced himself to consider other possibilities. "Maybe it was a wedding gift, Nora."

"No, the car with the vanity license plates that read Number One Daughter was my wedding gift. Geoff got one, too, only his was a Mercedes SL convertible with the plates NO1-SIL, for—you guessed it—Number One Son-in-Law. No, they did this deliberately."

Okay, Sam conceded privately, maybe they had. The question was why. Given the extensive search her father had under way for Nora, she was clearly loved very much. And, typically, fathers did not go around deliberately hurting children they loved very much.

Still trying to find a way to make peace between Nora and her father, the way she had tried to alleviate the tension between himself and his younger sister, Sam tried a different approach. "Maybe Geoff and your father meant well, but didn't tell you because they knew how you'd react to such a generous gift from your father to Geoff," he theorized gently.

Nora rolled her eyes and, shoving both hands through her hair, began to pace. "'No duh' to that!"

Sam fell in behind her. When she stopped at the sink, and turned to stare gloomily out the window at the mixture of snow and sleet still raining down from the sky, he lifted his hands to her shoulders. Feeling the tenseness of her muscles, beneath the warmth of her skin, he kneaded her muscles gently.

"Maybe it was a surprise for you," he continued, in an effort to make her feel better and come to grips with what had happened to literally send her running out into the cold. "Maybe your dad thought bringing Geoff into the company would make you happy."

Nora whirled around so swiftly she collided with his chest. "No, he knew I'd object," she disagreed firmly, looking up at him "That's why they didn't tell me."

Ignoring Nora's dark warning look, Sam stared down into the flushed contours of her face. "Did they actually say this to you?" he demanded.

Nora tossed her mane of hair and propped her fists on her slender hips. Tilting her head back, she continued to stare up at him irately—irritated that, right or wrong, he hadn't automatically taken her side. "We didn't discuss it," she told him tersely. "I heard them going over the terms of the agreement, line by line, item by item, just the way you do in any complicated business agreement. Then I saw Geoff smile like he couldn't wait to collect his payoff and pick up the pen to sign it." Nora paused abruptly, the humiliation she'd felt explicit in her eyes. She swallowed hard and continued, in a low, husky voice, "So I wrote a note telling everyone the marriage was off, and then I left," she concluded in a low, anguished tone.

Sam admired the fact that Nora was strong enough to do what she felt she had to do in any given situation. He didn't like the fact that she had run away before giving anyone a chance to state the reasons behind their actions, or say why they felt justified in doing so. Two wrongs did not make a right. They never had and never would.

"Well, that explains why your dad is so frantic," Sam sighed. It didn't explain why Geoff did not appear to be at least equally involved in the search for his missing fiancée, Sam thought. If he had been in Geoff's shoes, he would have gone to the ends of the earth to protect Nora, and to ensure her happiness. He certainly would not have accepted a lucrative gift from her family when he knew—as Geoff had to know—it would hurt Nora so. Sam didn't care what the business or familial rationale was.

Nora pouted and placed her hands square on Sam's

chest. "Fine. My father's frantic. I'm hurt. End of story."

She pushed as if to expand her personal space and move him away from her, but Sam stayed where he was—trapping her between him and the counter—and refused to budge until he'd said everything that needed to be said. "You need to fix things with your dad, Nora," he told her sternly.

Nora released a furious sigh and turned her head to the side, away from his passionately imploring gaze. "Sam, stay out of this," she told him, reminding him that when threatened she never gave an inch without a fight.

He cupped her chin with his hand and turned her face to his. Her soft body trembled against the length of his as he warned, "It'll haunt you if you don't. Call him."

Nora regarded him cantankerously, refusing to back down. "No."

"Then promise me you'll at least think about calling him."

Nora shook her head and remained adamantly opposed.

Frustrated, Sam kept her eyes on the flushed contours of her face and tried another approach. "If you don't, you know someone else is going to eventually see one of the flyers they've had printed up and collect the reward."

She scoffed and regarded him with a derisiveness that made his heart pound all the harder. "Who—you?"

Doing his best to ignore the compelling drift of her

floral perfume and the soft warmth of her body, where it pressed up against his, Sam swore curtly. "Dammit, Nora, you know money isn't my interest here." *You are.*

"Then what is?" she returned, just as shortly.

"Taking care of you—and your family."

Nora shook her head and pushed away from Sam. "I understand you take your job as community peacemaker seriously, and wish your parents were still alive. But my situation is different, Sam." She spun around to face him. "If I call my father, we'll argue. Trust me. That is not going to make either of us happy. Then he'll track me down, using your phone number. And we'll all be even more unhappy."

Sam closed the distance between them and took her all the way into his arms. "He's going to track you down, anyway," he told her silkily. "Why not get it over with? Why not contact him first, on your terms?" he asked softly, tunneling his hands through the silk of her hair.

Nora went very still. She tilted her head back and studied him as relentlessly as he was surveying her. Her conflicting feelings on the subject were reflected in her dark green eyes. "You're not going to give up on this, are you, Sam?" she asked wearily at last, her slender body softening against his.

Sam shook his head and stroked a comforting hand down her back. Although he knew the timing was off, he wanted nothing more than to kiss her until all the hurt she felt went away—and stayed away. "You owe it to your father to at least let him know you're all right,'' Sam told her softly, lacing both his hands around her hips.

''Fine.'' Nora sighed in defeat as she slipped from his arms once again and bounded toward the kitchen phone. ''I'll call his office and leave a message on his voice mail.'' Apparently determined to get the unpleasant chore over with as swiftly as possible, Nora punched in a number, then waited impatiently until it was time to record a message.

''Daddy, this is Nora. I'm still angry with you, but I'm all right, so stop worrying about me and stop looking for me, and for heaven's sake, take that reward off my head! Because I am not coming home until I'm ready, and right now I don't know when that will be—if ever!'' Finished, Nora slammed down the phone and whirled toward him. She tossed her mane of dark hair and folded her arms in front of her. ''There!'' she said hotly, looking Sam up and down, her entire body seething with suppressed fury. ''I've done it!''

Sam grinned broadly, pleased he'd talked some sense into her, against all odds. Now that they'd made some headway on that score, it was time to work on getting the rest of Nora's life in order. And he knew just where to start in making her feel a lot less misunderstood and a lot more loved.

''I hope you're satisfied!'' Nora continued furiously, stalking past him.

Sam caught her by the hem of her sweatshirt, and brought her back around to face him. ''Not yet,'' he drawled playfully, sinking into a chair and pulling her down onto his lap, so that her gently rounded bottom contacted with the hardness of his thighs. "But I could be," he promised in mock seriousness.

"Really?" she queried defiantly, with a temper Sam found every bit as delicious as her kisses. "What else do you want?"

You, Nora, heart and soul, Sam thought. But, determined to keep it light and easy as they left their disagreement behind them and focused on the future, he placed his finger beneath her chin and pulled her face to his. "Given our agreement to take our attraction for each other all the way, I'd think that would be obvious." He lowered his mouth to hers, felt her soft gasp, felt her tense in anticipation. And still the desire in her was nothing compared to his. "I want this."

Sam kissed Nora, letting his feelings take over as the kiss edged toward desperation. Nora did not pull away until his hand moved toward her breasts, and then she did pull away—decisively. "You're saying you want us to make love—now—just like that?" Nora said, her face assuming a panicked look that spoke even more eloquently of her lack of bedroom experience than her previous statements on the subject.

"No," Sam said softly, knowing that Nora was one woman who would take lots of careful handling and tender loving care, if she was to achieve the satisfaction she deserved, but he was more than up to the task. Given half a chance, he knew, he could make her happier than she had ever been—in bed and in life.

"Most definitely not just like that, Nora," Sam told

Nora softly, commiserating with her sudden case of nerves as he sifted his hands through the silken ends of her hair. "I want us to make love." He drew back and looked into her face. "But only when we're both ready, and the time is right for both of us."

Nora jerked in a breath as her emerald-green eyes darkened with a mixture of anxiety and pleasure. He knew she was oblivious to the way her sweatshirt clung to her breasts, delineating the softly rounded globes, but he sure wasn't.

Her arms clung softly to his shoulders as she told him with wry self-deprecation, "I'm not sure I'm experienced enough to figure that out, Sam."

A very primitive, very male satisfaction rushed through Sam as he scooped her closer and positioned her against his chest. Maybe it was the Neanderthal in him, but he was glad her experience in the bedroom was limited. He wanted to be the first to show her. He closed his eyes and, just for a moment, touched his lips to her temple, inhaling the flowery scent of her hair and skin. "Trust me. We'll both know when the time is right," Sam promised as he bent to kiss her, in a soft, evocative way that soon had her nerves fading.

"And in the meantime, until it is—?" Nora queried, as she clung to him and their slow, languid kiss came to a halt.

"We'll take it slow and easy," Sam promised. "And concentrate on getting to know each other a little better." He grinned and, knowing he had better get her off his lap if he was to keep his promise, set her aside and rolled to his feet. He started for the dinner she'd been fixing, and also grabbed a bottle of wine from the rack. "Fortunately, since we've found ourselves snowed in, it won't be difficult to give each other our undivided attention." He gave her a teasing wink. "'Cause this evening, I want you to be all mine."

SAM was as good as his word, Nora swiftly realized as the two of them warmed bread and cheese in the microwave, opened a bottle of wine, added fruit to their dinner tray and then took it all into the living room to sit before the fire.

Soon they were talking about everything and anything, including the most intimate and rudimentary details of their lives.

"You know how and why I went into law enforcement," Sam told her after he put some soft music on the stereo. He returned to her side and, now that they were finished with their meal, poured them both some more wine. "What I don't know is how and why you happened to go into advertising."

Nora smiled as she turned her glance toward the snow and sleet pouring down outside, draping their entire world in a frosty white coating that left them feeling all the more warm and cozy cuddled inside by the fire. Thinking how handsome he looked in jeans and a casual sweater that brought out the golden-brown in his eyes, she sipped her wine and settled comfortably into the sofa cushions opposite him. They were turned so that they were facing each other, but close enough that her bent knee was pressed comfortably against his rock hard thigh.

Nora sighed contentedly. She rested her bent elbow on the high back of the sofa, and propped her head on her upraised hand as she regarded Sam over the rim of her wineglass. "I always preferred the commercials to the programs." He lifted a brow, intrigued, prompting her to confess smugly, "By the time I was four, I could dance and sing the jingle to every product in my mother's shopping basket." The playfulness of his glance warmed her from head to toe and sent a curious thrill through her. Setting her glass aside, she propped a hand on her hip and regarded him with mock indignation. "I can see you find that hard to believe."

Sam flattened a hand across his chest comically. "Did I say that?"

"You don't have to," Nora replied dryly, knowing him well enough to realize where his thoughts were headed. "Not to worry, though. We can easily put my outrageous claim to the test."

"How?"

"By playing name that jingle, of course."

"What's the prize?" Sam's eyes darkened with mischief.

"Whatever you want, if you win. Whatever I want, if I win."

Sam put his own glass aside and regarded her with a smile that let her know that when it came to games and one-upmanship in a battle-of-the-sexes way, he was every bit the competitor she was. "You're on, woman."

"Okay," Nora said, trying not to notice how soft and touchable his golden-brown hair looked in the firelight. "I get to go first. You get two clues of any kind about the advertisement in question, and then you have to name the product. Ready?"

His grin widened speculatively. "As I'll ever be."

"Okay. The *1812 Overture*—" Nora hummed a few bars of the famous music "—and a cannon."

Sam snapped his fingers in recognition and quickly blurted out, "Quaker Puffed Oats."

Uh-oh. Nora regarded Sam with respect. She hadn't been sure he'd get that one. Now that he had, she wondered what he would claim as his prize. She made a face. "You're better than I anticipated."

"Does that mean I win?" he asked hopefully, turning sideways on the sofa.

Nora nodded reluctantly, her heart racing at the distinctly sexual intent she saw in his eyes. She wet her lips nervously. "Round one goes to you." She paused, afraid she already knew the answer. "What do you want for your prize?"

Sam's gaze roved her lazily. "Three guesses." He drew her into the apex of his legs, clasped her against his chest and tilted her face up to his. Then his mouth was on hers, and she was swept up into a kiss that was shattering in its possessive sensuality. He kissed her as though he were in love with her. He kissed her as though he meant to have her. And the taste of him, so hot and dark and male, set off a firestorm of sensation within her. Yearning spiraled through her, and she made a soft, helpless sound in the back of her throat. When he finally lifted his head, her heart was pounding, and there was a definite telltale weakness in her knees.

"Ready to give up?" he teased.

"Without a fight? Never." As his eyes glimmered playfully, Nora put a palm against his chest. "Besides, we digress. It's your turn to give me two clues."

"Okay."

It stunned Nora—the commercial expert—to realize that he already had one ready.

"Aaron Copland's *Appalachian Spring*—" Sam paused to hum a few bars of the familiar melody "—and a white china plate."

"What's for dinner?" Nora paraphrased the commercial's slogan triumphantly. "Beef."

Sam looked at her as appreciatively as if she were Venus emerging from the sea. "You're good," he murmured as he ran his fingers through the silken ends of her hair. "Round two goes to you."

"Yes, well, that was easy," Nora said modestly as she drew a bolstering breath. "It's current."

"What do you want as your prize?" Sam asked.

"Mmm, good question," Nora replied playfully, really beginning to get into the game. Determined to outdo the impact he'd had on her, she unbuttoned his shirt and smoothed her hand sensually over his chest. The golden mat of hair was soft and curly. Beneath the smooth skin and hard muscle, she felt the racing of his heart.

Able to see that she was getting to him even more than he'd gotten to her, she drew back. Withdrew her hand.

"That's it?" he asked hoarsely. Letting her know

with a glance that if it'd been his turn, he would've done a whole lot more.

"That's it," Nora said softly. And it had been enough, because just touching him that way—once—had made her want him more.

His expression tortured, Sam sat back breathlessly. "Okay, your turn."

With effort, Nora forced all thoughts of Sam and wild, passionate lovemaking from her mind, and—getting back into the spirit of the game, and out of her increasingly rich fantasies—she hummed a little ditty that had been around for years. "Plus, a man in a T-shirt, carrying a bucket," she said, when she'd finished the tune.

"Mr. Clean," Sam announced triumphantly, moving so that his back was to the sofa and Nora was seated firmly on his lap, facing him. "And it's my turn to collect," he murmured as he framed her face with his hands.

Surprised at his audacity—for there was no way she could not feel the rigid proof of his arousal pressing against her softness—Nora muttered a breathless "Sam!"

"Ah-ah-ah!" He grinned. "Not until I've had my prize." He aligned their lips with earth-shattering precision and gave her another long, thorough kiss, his hand sliding under her sweater, past her ribs and around her back. And he kept on kissing her until there was no denying the feelings swirling around inside her. She wanted him, needed him, needed this, and that knowledge lent an edge to an already dangerous evening.

When he released her, Nora realized something was definitely amiss. If she was right in her assessment of the situation, he was definitely very smooth, she decided, as warm sensations gathered in her breasts. "Did you just unsnap my bra?" she asked, deciding just for the heck of it *not* to immediately rectify the situation.

"Looks like, doesn't it?" He grinned mischievously. "And it's my turn to give the clues. I don't think this commercial has a song, at least I don't recall one, but the ad has a little boy named Mikey and a bowl of cereal nobody wants."

"That's easy," Nora murmured. "Life cereal."

"Correct again."

Nora studied him, wondering if she should go for the expected—or unexpected—kiss, or more touching, or do something more daring yet. She knew what she wanted. His hands, gently caressing her breasts.

Sam studied her face. "Uh-oh, I'm in trouble now, aren't I?" he teased softly.

Nora smiled and said, "I'm just thinking how I'm going to collect my prize." The decision to be daring made, she took his hands, settled them on her rib cage, beneath her sweater, then wreathed her arms about his neck and ever-so-slowly leaned into him. Their lips met in another free fall of sensation. Then need took over once again, making them both reckless and relentless. He cupped her breasts, teasing her nipples into peaks with his thumbs and forefingers and laving them with his tongue. She caressed his chest. The next thing she knew, they were prone on the sofa.

He was lying with one leg draped between hers and kissing her like there was no tomorrow.

Eventually, she recalled they were supposed to be playing a game. "Whose turn is it?" Nora asked breathlessly as an arrow of fire shot through her and she arched against him, burying her hands in his hair.

Sam ran a hand down her thigh as he gathered her close. "I think we're sharing this one."

SHARING, indeed, Nora thought as Sam's lips covered hers once again and she lost her breath at the renewed probing of his tongue. She might be new at this, she thought dizzily as she kissed him deeply and tenderly, but Sam knew exactly what to do. And while she didn't know exactly what the rest of her life held, right now she didn't care. All that mattered was that the chance to be with Sam like this might never come again. If she didn't take advantage of it, she'd regret it forever, and she didn't want regrets where the two of them were concerned, only sweet, wonderful memories.

Only this, she thought as everything around her went soft and fuzzy, except for the hot, sizzling pressure of his mouth on hers. With a low moan of satisfaction, his expression fierce with longing and the primal need to possess, Sam cupped her face and angled her head so that their kiss could deepen even more. Her heart pounding, the need in her an incessant ache, she arched against him, her body moving in undulations.

The fullness of him straining against her thigh, he lifted the hem of her sweatshirt, trailing the soft, cozy fleece across her skin and exposing her rosy-tipped breasts to his rapacious view. He bent his head, his lips tracing a fiery erotic path across the swell of flesh.

The slow, hot strokes of his tongue across her nipples were unbearably tender, intimate and seductive. Helpless to resist, Nora arched into his touch. She closed her eyes as the fragrance of his aftershave, so brisk and wintry, filled her senses and the sandpapery feel of his evening beard sensually abraded her skin. This was heaven, Nora thought. Certainly, the closest she'd ever come. And they hadn't even come close to making love!

"Oh, God, Nora, I want you," Sam murmured, shifting upward and fitting his mouth over hers again. To know that she wanted him was exciting. To know that she'd surrendered sent him over the edge. "I want you so much," he whispered breathlessly against her mouth.

Eager to please him as he was pleasing her, she slid her hands beneath the layers of cotton molding his torso and caressed the smoothly muscled skin of his chest, shoulders and back. His flat male nipples pebbled beneath her palms. Lower still, the unmistakable evidence of his arousal pressed between her thighs. And all the while, she couldn't believe how he was making her feel. She never wanted it to stop, never.

And Sam evidently knew it, too, as he tugged off her pants and she helped with his jeans. The rest of their clothing soon followed. She felt deliciously light-headed as he stretched out naked beside her, watching her face as he flattened one hand beneath her hips and arched her lower body close to his. Her toes curled, she was aroused to the point of distraction, and still—still—he was taking his sweet, sweet time, stroking her dewy softness, moving up, in.

Sam settled over her, the tip of his manhood pressing against her delicate folds. Nora moved to receive him. He pushed upward, gentle and slow, and met unexpected resistance. She tensed as he tried again, even more tenderly, then stopped in shock. Eyes full of wonder and fiercely masculine possessiveness, he stared down at her, knowing, it seemed, what she'd never come out and exactly said. "Nora—"

Nora didn't need a crystal ball to know what he was thinking, to know he was about to do the gallant thing. She clutched his shoulders and urged him closer, knowing the moment, the man, were all finally right. Looking into his eyes, she nestled against him, marveling at the need she had created in him, a need she could ease. "Just love me, Sam," she whispered, knowing she wanted to feel every tremble, every gasp. "That's all I ask."

She clasped the smooth, warm muscles of his back. His body trembling with the effort it took to contain his own pressing need, Sam surged upward, smoothly and deliberately penetrating the final barrier.

Fulfillment flowing through her, for at last she was finding out what all the books and movies and songs were about, Nora surged against him. "That's it." Sam whispered his encouragement, lifting her hips and deepening his penetration even more. "Take all of me, Nora," Sam whispered, still kissing her deeply, "all of me."

She didn't think she could, and then, suddenly, she had.

Desire both driving and overwhelming her, she arched up to meet him, new demand welling up inside of her. She couldn't get enough of him. No one had ever kissed her like this. No one had ever demanded or given as much. Moaning softly, she wrapped her arms around him and urged him on. Her heart soaring—for this was her wildest dream and her most romantic fantasy come true—she closed her eyes as a hunger unlike any she had ever known built inside her.

Anchoring her against him, Sam moved deeper and deeper inside her, his thorough possession and sweet, invigorating kisses making her want, making her moan, making her need. Until at last their control faltered and all was lost in a blazing whirlwind of mutual heat and release. Nora shuddered, and with a hoarse cry, he surged inside her.

AFTERWARD, Sam wrapped them in a blanket and cuddled with Nora on the sofa before the fire. He stroked her hair and held her close and thought about seeing her in that white dress. From the first moment he laid eyes on her, he had known she was the kind of woman he could fall in love with, as well as someone very special. She was so beautiful and sensual. Even when she hinted at her lack of experience, he'd had no idea how deep her innocence went.

Loving the way she snuggled against him, he curved his arm around her protectively and gently stroked her arm. "Why didn't you tell me you'd never made love before?"

Nora shook her head, embarrassed. Turning toward him, she buried her face in the curve of his shoulder. "It's going to sound corny if I tell you," she murmured shyly as she traced patterns in the whorling hair on his chest.

Sam smiled and gently kissed the top of her head. "That's okay," he whispered tenderly, drawing her closer yet. "I like corny. And I really want to know."

Nora sighed and turned her gaze to the crackling embers of the fire. "It goes back to something my mother told me when I was growing up," she said affectionately. "She said making love was the most special thing in the world between a man and a woman, and that I shouldn't squander it. She said I would know in my heart when everything...the time...the man...the moment...was right, and that I should wait until it was and not push myself into something I wasn't ready for."

Sam smiled as he studied the proud, beautiful contours of Nora's face. "Wise woman, your mother."

"Yes." Nora sighed contentedly, her body softening all over again as she rolled onto her back. "She was."

Sam shifted so that he was looking down into her face. "I wish you'd told me," he said as he stroked her cheek.

Nora shrugged and lifted shimmering eyes to his. She paused and bit her lip. "I wasn't sure it mattered all that much."

"You have to know it does," Sam said hoarsely.

For it told him she hadn't gone into this love affair with him lightly. Nor, for all their talk of flings, had he.

Nora's eyes lit with a tender glow, and she gently touched his face. "This was special for me, Sam," she told him softly. "So very special."

Sam buried his face in her hair and held her close, knowing in his heart that Nora was not the only one whose life had been transformed tonight. "For me, too."

Chapter Eleven

Sam lay awake long after Nora fell asleep. He kept thinking about Nora's dad. Charles Kingsley's anguish had really gotten to him. Maybe because he knew that if he was in Charles's place he would be going out of his mind with worry, wondering if Nora was all right.

Sam knew Nora was angry. If all she'd told him was factually correct—and not, as Sam hoped, a misunderstanding that could be cleared up as soon as Nora and Charles hashed things out—she had a right to be ticked off. It still wasn't right for Nora to worry her father like that—particularly when the snowstorm of the century was raging across the entire northeastern United States. Whether Nora liked it or not, her father deserved to know she was safe, and would continue to be, as long as she stayed in Clover Creek.

Knowing that his conscience would not let him rest until he acted to calm the fears of Nora's dad, Sam eased from the bed, grabbed his robe from the hook on the bathroom door and went downstairs.

Charles Kingsley sighed his relief as soon as Sam finished bringing him up-to-date on Nora's whereabouts. "Thank you for letting me know she's all right. I'll make arrangements to get the reward to you as soon as possible."

"I don't want a reward," Sam explained patiently, being careful to keep his voice low as he moved closer to the dying embers of the fire. Cradling the phone against his ear, he knelt to add another log. "I'm doing this for Nora. I think she needs to make peace with you more than she knows right now."

"I hope you're right about that," Charles replied. "If you could put her on the phone, I'd like to speak with her."

As much as Sam wanted to do that, he knew Nora was not ready to deal with Charles. Willing to do whatever it took to protect Nora, Sam said politely, "She needs a little time."

Charles sighed heavily. "You know, I lost her mother some years ago...."

"Yes, I do." And Sam was sorry about that, but it didn't change the situation now.

A poignant silence fell. "I'm afraid I'm going to lose Nora, too," Charles continued thickly at last.

"You're going to have to be patient with her," Sam advised.

He shot a look at the stairs. He noted with relief that there were no signs of activity coming from the loft bedroom, but, leery of waking Nora with his voice, he replaced the fireplace screen and took the portable phone and moved toward the kitchen. "Your daughter's been through a lot, and she's still reeling." Sam knew better than anyone how vulnerable she was to hurt. He would have laid down his life to protect her.

"I'll try," Charles replied, aggrieved. "But you don't know what you're asking. Nora's all I've got."

And all I want, Sam thought as he paced back and forth. *All I've ever wanted*. Which made it all the more important that he succeed in reuniting Nora and Charles.

"This will all work out," Sam said determinedly, "if you just give Nora a little space to recoup and some time for her temper to cool down. In the meantime, you don't need to worry about your daughter's personal safety. My family and I'll watch over her while she's in Clover Creek." And in the process, he would do everything he could to make sure he and Nora were together, not just for the next few days, but forever.

Charles paused thoughtfully. "You'll let me know as soon as Nora is willing to talk with me?"

"Absolutely," Sam promised. He was glad he'd made this overture. He felt better. So did Charles. And soon—he hoped—Nora would, too. In the meantime, he'd done all he could for tonight.

The two men promised to keep in touch, albeit surreptitiously. Charles thanked Sam for getting in touch with him. And the two men said goodbye. As Sam hung up the phone, he heard soft footsteps behind him. He turned just as Nora padded into the kitchen. Barefoot, tousled, she was wearing only his shirt. His eyes drifting over her long, lissome legs, Sam realized he had never seen her look sexier. His lower body throbbed in reaction, even as the rest of him tensed with guilt.

Still approaching him languidly, she rubbed her eyes and stifled a yawn. "Were you on the phone just now?" she asked softly.

Sam nodded as Nora glided into his arms and rested her head on his shoulder. "Everything okay?" she continued, in a deeply concerned voice that made him feel all the guiltier for going behind her back, even if it was for her own good.

"I think it will be, when this storm lets up," Sam confided as he wrapped his arms around her and felt the soft give of her body next to his.

Nora cuddled against him. "Good. Then come back to bed," she urged gently, running her fingers through his hair. She stood on tiptoe to press her lips to his. "Because I've missed you."

Sam grinned. He could tell by the way she laced her arms around his neck and molded her body to his that this was all too true. And, more, that she was as eager for more loving as he was. "Really?" he drawled, wrapping his arms around her. Pulling her against him, he delivered a long, steamy kiss that soon had them both trembling and his heart racing as blood rushed into his groin.

As they drew apart, slowly and reluctantly, Nora tucked one hand in his, and used the other to tug on the belt of his robe. "Come back upstairs with me," she promised with an impish grin, "and I'll show you how much."

"WELL?" Nora asked the following morning, as Sam ventured off the porch of his A-frame to get more wood for the fireplace.

Sam grinned as his footsteps crunched beneath him, but did not penetrate the thick white layer on the ground. Six inches of hard-as-a-rock sleet was on top of the eighteen inches of snow they had already had. "It's like walking on a tundra," he announced cheerfully.

Nora planted both hands on her slender hips and regarded the crusty layer skeptically. "It *looks* like the frost that forms on the inside of a freezer."

Sam held out a gloved hand to her and urged her to come out and play. "You'll never know what it feels like unless you come on out and give it a try," he beckoned teasingly.

"You're sure I won't sink through?" she asked worriedly, tucking her gloved hand into the warmth and safety of his.

"I haven't." Sam grinned, and delicious lights sparkled in his eyes, reminding her of all they'd shared the night before. She might have been sexually inexperienced, but she knew that what they shared had been a lot more than just passion. They'd connected, heart and soul, in a way that was very special. The trick would be to hang on to that feeling, and build on it, again and again and again, until they had a love that neither of them could ever turn their back on.

Nora smiled. "True," she said. Knowing she'd trust him with her life, Nora allowed Sam to help her down the porch steps, onto the ground. "This is so weird," she said as she stepped experimentally over the rough layer of frosty white, "but it's not nearly as slippery as I would've expected it to be, given that the top layer of it is ice." Nora turned to Sam. "So, how long do you think it's going to stay this way?" she asked, as casually as possible, aware that she wanted more than anything for them to remain stranded together a lot longer than she sensed they ultimately would be.

"The weather report on the radio just now said they don't expect it to start thawing until tomorrow."

Thank heaven for small miracles! Nora thought. "And the snowplows...?"

"Are out," Sam affirmed, tenderly brushing the hair from her cheek. "They're not having much luck, though, 'cause you really need a pickax to break through this, so all the roads, including the interstate, are closed for now."

Which meant she was still stuck here. "What about you?" she asked cheerfully. "Are you going to be able to get in to work today at all?"

Sam shook his head. "My deputies are going to cover for me until I can get back to town tomorrow. Fortunately, things are pretty quiet."

Nora cast a look at the brilliant blue sky overhead. She didn't see a cloud in sight. "Are we expecting any more snow?"

"Nope." One hand around her waist, Sam tugged her passionately close and whispered in her ear, "The snowstorm of the century has officially left West Virginia. It's bearing down on New England now."

"So we're stuck here, hmm?" Nora tried not to notice how good it felt to be in his arms again or how proprietorially he had splayed his hand across her back.

"Until the warm front gets here tomorrow and everything starts to melt," Sam affirmed.

Nora had only to look at Sam to know he wanted to make love to her again and again—all day. "I feel like a kid playing hooky from school," she murmured, as a warm flush started in her tummy and crept upward.

Sam grinned and urged her closer with the flat of his hand. "Me too."

Nora blushed as the fluttering in her tummy slipped a little lower. The prospect of so much intimate time with Sam made her spirits soar and her heart beat a little harder. The worry over where this would all lead, however, still made her feel that some caution was in order.

In the heat of passion, she'd told Sam she could handle a winter-storm-induced fling, and indeed, she had wanted just that, with all her heart and soul. This morning, with the snow and sleet no longer pouring down from the sky above, the bitingly cold air assaulting her senses and the sun shining brightly overhead, things looked a little different.

This morning, she could not deny that she felt more for Sam than simple lust. The question was, what did he feel for her? Was she going to end up being even more hurt by this affair with him than she had been by either Geoff or her father? Nora hoped not, but she could not—in all honesty—be sure she would leave here with her heart intact. Knowing, however, that it was too soon to be talking about any of this,

Nora marshaled her emotions from his probing gaze and turned away. "It's nice out here," she remarked pleasantly.

Sam studied her, as if struggling with the effort not to discuss certain things, too, for fear of ruining the mood. After a pause, he probed gruffly, "You don't find it too quiet for you?"

Nora shook her head and smiled. About that, she was able to be perfectly open and honest. "After years of living in the city, I cherish the peace and quiet. You must, too."

"More than you know," he said teasingly as he swept her up into his arms, bent her backward from the waist and abruptly took her lips with the complete, unrestrained physicality she had always craved but had never experienced until last night.

Nora reveled in the impact he had on her senses, and the even more devastating effect he had on her heart. Maybe an affair—however short-lived, was not such a bad idea, Nora thought optimistically. Maybe an affair *this* passionate would lead to something else. Like love. Marriage. A home and children of their own. At least, Nora thought a little dazedly, as Sam's mouth knowingly contoured to hers, expertly staking his claim, it felt like it would....

Long minutes later, as the tempestuous kiss came to an end, Nora moaned and sagged against him, the bulk of her weight resting against his bent knee. "See what I mean?" Sam teased, looking—for a moment—every bit as lovestruck and mesmerized as she felt whenever she was with him.

Nora sighed contentedly, knowing it was obvious,

whether she wanted to admit it or not. "You're very naughty, Sam Whittaker. You're making me never want to leave."

Satisfied male laughter rumbled in his chest. "After last night, that's the general idea," he drawled, his lips lingering seductively over the nape of her neck. He drew back, the promise in his eyes and the tenderness of his touch combining to hold her spellbound.

Nora knew that if she was going to err, it should be on the side of caution, but there was just something about the hard, warm body aligned with hers that made him impossible to resist. He was just so determined to make her his; she knew he wouldn't let anything stand in his way. And that pleased her more than she could ever say. She had always wanted to be desired in exactly this way.

"And since you've brought it up," he drawled, as a slow smile lit his eyes and he righted her slowly. "Why not give some thought to settling permanently in Clover Creek?"

"You're serious, aren't you?" Nora asked Sam as they trooped back inside to make something to eat.

Sam helped her off with her coat. "Very."

"To tell you the truth, I've been thinking about it. There's plenty of work here, and I like the people."

Sam cocked his head and gave her the thorough once-over. "Is that the only reason?"

"You know it's not." She mocked his smart-mouthed drawl to a tee.

Half his mobile mouth crooked up contemplatively, and they exchanged grins. Apparently, Nora thought, as she quickly put together some breakfast for them—the coffee he'd already prepared, juice and microwaved muffins—the physical side of their relationship was something they could easily deal with.

The emotional aspects were tricker, but maybe, with time, those would become easier to discuss, too. At least Nora hoped so.

"You know, I never thought I'd say this, but getting downsized out of my job is the best thing that's ever happened to me." Nora set everything on a tray and carried it into the living room. She set it on the coffee table in front of the sofa and continued confiding contentedly, "It forced me to reexamine my life, to reorder my priorities, and think about what has made me the happiest in this life."

"And that's what?" Sam asked seriously, as he added more logs to the fire, then came back to lounge beside her on the sofa.

"Family," Nora replied, memories assailing her, as she perched on the edge of the sofa and served them both. "When my mom was alive, before she got sick and my dad got so overprotective, we were really happy. And content. I want that again," she told Sam as she handed him his coffee and the connection of their hands sent a sweet, sexy warmth zinging through her. "I want what you have," she told Sam softly.

"Which is...?"

Plate balanced on her lap, Nora settled back beside him. "A family who loves you deeply and yet doesn't constantly try to manipulate or control you." She sighed wistfully and shook her head, then lifted her coffee cup to her lips. "I want to be surrounded by people who won't constantly meddle in my life and try to make all my decisions for me.''

At Nora's innocently uttered wish, Sam felt a flicker of guilt. He wondered how Nora would react if she knew he'd already called her father for her and let Charles Kingsley know where she was, as well as meddled a bit in order to get Nora's father to give Nora a little of the time to recoup that she so desperately needed. He knew he'd done the right thing—the only thing—but would she see it that way? He had the sinking feeling that she wouldn't.

''And—'' Nora sipped her juice and continued contentedly, oblivious to Sam's fears ''—I want a home in a nice, safe place, and children, *and* my very own advertising agency.''

Resisting the urge to take her in his arms and hold her close, Sam tucked a strand of hair behind her ear. ''That's not so much to wish for.''

Nora paused, and a troubled look came back into her eyes. ''Maybe not.'' She set her glass aside, took a tremulous breath and released it slowly. ''But for a long time I've lived with the feeling that at any moment the rug could be pulled out from under me again, like it was after my mother's death, and when I lost my job, and found out how Geoff had gone behind my back to draw up the prenup with my father. And that scares me, Sam.'' She paused and looked up at him, her dark green eyes glimmering with unshed tears. ''It scares me so much. I don't ever want to feel lost and alone like that again. And at the same time—'' she bit into her lower lip to stop it from trembling "—I don't want to feel like I can never rely on anyone but myself, either."

"You have to know, if it were me, if I were the man in your life, I would never leave you," Sam said quietly, wishing he could erase her hurt.

The tears she'd been defiantly holding back spilled past her lashes and slipped down her face. "I want it to be that way," she whispered, turning to face him.

Clamping his hands on her waist, Sam shifted her onto his lap and held her close. "Then believe it," he whispered back, kissing her deeply and stroking her hair, knowing he would do literally anything and everything to protect her, whether she asked him to or not, "'cause it's true."

They kissed again, and cuddled together, each of them thinking how best to resolve her situation so that Nora would be free to concentrate on her own life, their romance and the future Sam wanted with her. "Maybe if you called your dad and talked to him this time—" Sam suggested finally, "instead of just leaving a message on a machine, you could make things right between you and your father again."

Nora sighed and made a regretful face, a discouraged look coming into her eyes as she bounced from Sam's lap and began to pace the room. "I've tried, Sam. But my father never listens to me. He always just tells me what he thinks I should do, or think, or feel. And if I don't do what he thinks I should, he goes behind my back and arranges things anyway." She crossed her arms in front of her and finished stormily, "It's as if he thinks he can manage my life by decree."

Sam rolled to his feet and determinedly closed the distance between them. "I accept that your dad's meddling bothers you, Nora." Sam cupped her shoulders with his palms and turned her to face him. He knew, even if Nora didn't, that this was not a simple case of rebellion or miscommunication. Nora had been hurt by her father, for years now; she wasn't going to be really, truly happy until those hurts were resolved. And that, in turn, meant putting her many tempestuous defenses aside.

"What's harder for me to accept," Sam continued softly, "is you not being willing to try again to find a way to change things between the two of you, while you still have a chance to do so."

Nora lifted her chin and gazed deep into his eyes. The defiant edge was back in her voice as she asked, "Are we talking about me now, or you?"

"Maybe a little bit of both," Sam admitted honestly, aware that he was opening up to Nora in a way he hadn't opened up to anyone in a very long time. And there was a good reason for that. He wanted to be as close to her emotionally as he was physically. He wanted her to understand him as thoroughly as he longed to understand her.

He paused, marshaling his own feelings into a rock-hard resolve. "I've told you how much I regret the opportunities I lost to be close to my parents. I can't get those back, Nora," he explained, in a low voice laced with regret. "You, on the other hand, still have time to be with your dad and work things out." That wasn't something she should give up without a fight.

They studied each other in poignant silence. Finally, Nora uttered a soft, defeated sigh. "It means that much to you for me to call him?" she queried wearily, raking her hands through her hair.

"Yes, it does." Sam braced his shoulder on the mantel and tipped his head down at her. He paused a moment to let his words sink in. "I think, at the very least, you should see him and let him explain what he was trying to accomplish with that prenuptial agreement. There might be a lot more to it than you think."

"All right. I'll do it." Nora sighed. "I'll give my father a chance to explain. But not until tomorrow," she stipulated stubbornly, then followed that with a deep, intimate kiss that sent heat soaring through them both.

"Because today is ours, Sam, and I won't let anyone or anything interfere with that."

Chapter Twelve

Nora woke to the scraping sound of a snow shovel hitting the driveway. She got dressed quickly and made her way downstairs, where she donned her boots and coat and joined Sam outside. "It feels warmer," she said, looking up at the clear blue sky.

"It is—thirty-six degrees. The temperature rose overnight and made the snow soft enough for me to start digging us out with something other than a pickax."

"So we'll be able to get back to town today?" Nora didn't know whether to feel happy or sad about that. She only knew she had wanted their storm-generated romantic interlude to go on forever.

Sam nodded and smiled down at her. "I've already talked to the Clover Creek road and maintenance crew." He set his shovel aside. Wrapping both hands around her waist, he brought her close, so that her body was cradled in the solid warmth of his. "They're going to have a snowplow out this way by ten, so I want to get my truck dug out and driveway cleared so we can get back." Briefly, regret tinged his gaze. He lowered his mouth to hers and delivered a brief but oh-so-soulful kiss. "I hate to leave here, too," he murmured affectionately at last, "but I've got to relieve my deputies."

Nora nodded her understanding as she drank in the tantalizing fragrance of his skin. She and Sam had only known each other since the blizzard began, yet during that brief time she had felt more challenged, cherished and loved than she ever had. She hated to think what the return to normal weather and normal life might mean for their romance. With effort, she pushed her disturbing worries away; the end of the storm did not mean the end of their love affair. "Have you eaten breakfast?" she asked cheerfully. If not, Sam had to be ravenous, after all this physical activity.

Sam shook his head. He stroked his thumb across her cheek and looked into her eyes. "Made coffee, though."

"I'll make you something, then." Something special. Nora ran a possessive hand down his arm, savoring this time they had left. "When would you like to eat?"

"In an hour or so." Sam smiled, his happiness as potent and life-enriching as hers. "As soon as I'm finished here."

Nora went back inside, showered and dressed, wondering all the while whether anyone would know the changes she'd gone through in the past twenty-four hours. She knew that, with the exception of the flush of happiness in her cheeks and the new glimmer of excitement in her eyes, she looked the same. The problem was, she didn't feel the same. Being with

Sam had opened her up to the kind of passion she'd never dreamed existed. And it had shown her that the stronger a man was, the more tender and understanding he was, too. To the point that, after loving Sam, Nora knew she would never be the same again. And that, too, was all for the good, she thought contentedly, because she wanted to feel this way forever.

Finished, she made the bed where they'd slept, tidied the bathroom and went down to the kitchen. Glancing out the window, she saw that Sam was nearing the end of the driveway. Instead of clearing the whole thing, he had shoveled two long parallel paths that lined up with the tires.

Smiling at the way he wasted neither time nor energy, she got bacon strips ready to microwave and prepared hotcake batter for the griddle. It was almost ready when Sam came in. He shucked off his coat, hat, gloves and boots. Watching him wash up at the kitchen sink, Nora was filled with an odd kind of contentment. There was a pleasure in just being near him—a pleasure that she sensed was not going to go away, no matter how long she knew him.

They talked and laughed contentedly through the breakfast Nora had prepared.

Unfortunately, no sooner had they finished than the phone rang.

Sam got up to answer it. "Yeah. Hi, Gran. I'm glad to hear it. Yes, Nora and I are both fine. We're coming back to town as soon as the snowplow clears the farm-to-market road between here and town, which should be any minute now." As he listened intently, his eyes lit up. He covered the phone and spoke to her. "Gus just called. He's coming in and expects to be in Clover Creek around noon. He's still bringing a surprise with him. My grandparents are convinced it's a bride."

"Maybe it will be," Nora said, eyes sparkling.

Sam grinned, looking as if nothing would make him happier. "Maybe."

"I HATE TO SAY IT, but in this case, seeing is believing," Nora murmured as the parade of privately owned bright orange snowplows with Indiana license plates motored down the middle of Main Street and stopped in front of the Whittakers' store.

Sam shook his head, as always in awe of his older brother's penchant for flamboyance. "You can say that again," he drawled, watching as Gus and a beautiful young woman with an armful of flowers climbed down out of the first orange vehicle. An entire wedding party—and what Sam could only presume were some of the guests—followed, bringing with them champagne and even, incredibly, a four-tiered wedding cake. A photographer was madly snapping photos.

"Hey, everybody, I want you to meet Evelyn, my bride-to-be," Gus said, greeting his family and beaming from ear to ear.

"Nora! My goodness." Gus obviously had a million questions, but chose to ignore them. "You already know Evelyn, don't you?" Gus asked.

Nora nodded. She recognized Evelyn, from an L and B ad campaign for orange juice featuring the

USC women's volleyball team. "Hi," Nora said, greeting Evelyn and Gus both. "Congratulations."

"Thanks. What brings you to Clover Creek?" Gus asked Nora.

"Fate, and the blizzard, what else?" Nora quipped.

"Like it so far?" Gus asked.

"A lot," Nora said. And she meant that with all her heart.

"Congratulations, bro." Sam grinned and shook his brother's hand.

"We were so worried you wouldn't make it," Clara said as she enveloped Gus and Evelyn in warm hugs.

"Now, Gran," Gus drawled happily, "you knew I'd get here, even if I had to detour through several midwestern states to arrange it. After all, I couldn't get married without my family. I only hope the church is free."

"I'll call the reverend right now and find out!" Kimberlee said.

"I had a hankering for a candlelight ceremony this evening, at seven," Gus said.

"Then a candlelight ceremony it will be," Harold said.

"Meantime," Clara put in, taking charge, "we have a lot of work to do. So we all better get busy."

"I'VE SHARED YOU with everyone else long enough," Sam murmured, hours later, as he led Nora onto the dance floor and took her into his arms. "This dance is mine." As Nora, looking flushed and radiant, flu-

idly matched her steps to his, Sam exhaled contentedly. "It seems ages since I've held you in my arms."

"I know," Nora said teasingly. "And yet it's only
been a matter of hours."

"Even so," Sam said, aware that he'd never seen
her looking more beautiful than she did in the calf-
length off-the-shoulder green velvet dress that clung
to her soft breasts and slender hips, "that's way too
long."

"For me, too." Nora looked at his brother, then
back at him. "Gus and Evelyn really look happy."

Sam studied the beckoning depths of Nora's dark
green eyes. "I think they are."

"Kimberlee, too," Nora added softly.

Sam lifted their clasped hands to his lips and gently
kissed the fragrant softness of the back of her hand.
"That's because she talked to her boyfriend, Kenny,
again before the wedding. Apparently, he's coming
home for a visit in another week or two," Sam said.

Nora tilted her face up to Sam's. Her eyes were
inches from his, her lips even closer than that. All he
could think about was making slow, sweet love to her
again.

"I know Kimberlee's only seventeen, but I really
think she loves Kenny and believes she can't live
without him."

Sam nodded. Thanks to Nora, for the first time in
his life he was beginning to know exactly how his
younger sister felt. And while it did nothing to lessen
his responsibility to see that Kimberlee's education
was completed, her future assured, the surprising
depth of the feelings he had for Nora gave Sam a lot

more empathy for Kimberlee's situation. For the first time in his life, he knew what it was to want to be with someone as much as you needed to breathe, because that was how he felt about Nora.

"You seem deep in thought," Nora teased.

Sam sighed. "I was just thinking about the snowstorm of the century. I never believed a single blizzard could change my life irrevocably, but—" he bent and kissed her chastely, tenderly "—it has."

"For the better, I hope," Nora murmured, absently tracing the line of his jaw with the tip of her finger.

"You're damn right about that," Sam whispered back, pulling her closer. "I know it's just been a couple days, but my knowing you has made me richer in so many, many ways."

"Me too," Nora whispered back. "In fact, I was just thinking—" She stopped abruptly, her silky brow furrowing as the sound of the music playing on the rec hall's PA system was drowned out by the unmistakable sound of a helicopter close by.

"Is...that—?"

Sam frowned, knowing there had not been a police or medical emergency in the vicinity. If there had been, he, his two deputies and Doc Ellen—who was currently enjoying some punch and cake with her husband, Joe, and five-year-old daughter, Katie—would've all known about it, long before any lifeflight helicopter arrived. "That sounds like a chopper is setting down outside," Sam said.

For Gus's honeymoon, maybe? Sam wondered.

Before Sam could make his way to the exit to find out, the sound of the chopper ceased, the doors to the reception hall burst open and two men clad in elegant business attire strode in. Sam took in the familial resemblance of the distinguished, dark-haired fifty-something man to Nora, saw the much younger man with him, then glanced at the stricken look on Nora's face. It didn't take much detective work to put two and two together. "You weren't expecting to see your father this evening, I take it?" And was that the infamously jilted Geoff with him? Sam wondered.

"No. I wasn't." Nora's soft lips pursed mutinously, and she folded her slender arms in front of her.

Sam frowned. This was turning into a surprise for both of them. "I thought you were going to talk to your dad while I was at work today," Sam began. In fact, Nora had promised him as much during their drive back into town.

"I was." Nora picked up the nearly empty punch bowl and ducked into the adjacent rec hall kitchen as her father and his preppy-looking sidekick visually searched the crowded hall for her. "But then I got busy helping your grandmother and Kimberlee pull this wedding together for Gus and Evelyn and didn't have time." Nora's hands shook as she added more frozen lemonade, ice and lemon-lime soda to the bowl.

Sam knew Nora was only delaying the inevitable in not speaking to her father; nevertheless, his gut instinct was to protect Nora from hurt or distress of any kind. "You want me to head him off for you?" Nora's and Charles's first meeting could always be held later, after Sam had smoothed the way.

Nora stirred the punch vigorously. "If you wouldn't mind, yes, I'd appreciate it very much. The last thing I want is an emotional scene this evening."

Sam wasn't sure Nora was going to get her wish about that, but he headed for Charles Kingsley anyway.

"NORA?"

Nora turned around with a gasp. "Geoff!"

Geoff struck a distinguished pose in the small rec hall kitchen. "You're ticked off at me, aren't you?"

Nora flashed back to the sight of him discussing the prenup with her father, in the back of the church. She drew herself up indignantly, wondering how she had ever let herself be deceived that way. "What do you think?" she shot back coolly.

Geoff tugged at his necktie, as if it were strangling him. "Look, I don't know how you found out what your dad did to sort of speed our engagement along, but I had nothing to do with it!"

Nora glared at him. "I don't know how you can say that!"

"Because it's true," Geoff said sincerely, laying both hands across his chest. "And if you think about it, you'll know it's so, because I'm not the one with pull in the New York advertising world. Your dad is."

Nora blinked. "What are you talking about?" she asked incredulously.

"You—getting downsized out of a job in New York, so you'd have to come back to Pittsburgh and build a life there." Geoff paused. "We figured someone from L and B who'd come to the wedding had found out about it from the brass at L and B and told you before the wedding.''

''No, they didn't.'' If she'd known that, she never would have gone back, no matter what Sam or anyone else said!

Geoff continued to regard her uneasily. He swallowed hard, and then asked finally, ''Then what were you talking about just now?''

''The prenuptial agreement between you and my father!''

Geoff swore and paled even more. ''You knew about that, too?'' he asked incredulously.

''I saw you sign it, Geoff. I heard the two of you go over the terms in great detail, before the wedding.''

Beads of perspiration broke out on Geoff's upper lip as he muttered a silent prayer. ''Look, I can explain how and why that came about, Nora.''

''I'll just bet you can,'' Nora said sarcastically, ''but I don't want to hear it.'' She whirled and stomped off blindly, only to run headlong into Sam and her father. To Nora's increasing dismay, the two of them were not just talking. Her father was trying to push a check into Sam's hand.

''I insist,'' Charles Kingsley told Sam firmly, in a discreet voice that was nevertheless loud enough for both Nora and Geoff to hear. ''You've earned it. I couldn't have found my daughter anywhere near this quickly without you.''

FOR NORA, seeing the exchange of money behind her back was her worst nightmare all over again. Once again, she had been betrayed by the man she thought—hoped—she loved.

Oblivious to the music and laughter in the background, she stared at Sam incredulously. She wasn't sure whether to punch his lights out or burst into tears. She only knew she felt like doing both simultaneously. "Not you, too?" she whispered to Sam hoarsely as hot, angry tears filled her eyes. She couldn't believe he would manipulate, deceive and betray her this way. She'd thought he was different!

Looking more darkly handsome than ever in his tux, Sam spun around and regarded Nora grimly. "It's not what it looks like," he told her flatly.

A likely story. "Isn't it?" Nora presumed cooly.

"No," Sam replied firmly, shoving impatient fingers through his hair. "It isn't."

"Well, you could've fooled me," Nora muttered. "Or does the betrayal only count when you pay off in stock options and a piece of the family company?"

"For heaven's sake, Nora," Charles Kingsley said, interrupting sternly. "Sam did us a favor, in letting me know where you were."

"Maybe he did do one for you," Nora snapped back. "He did not do one for me." She whirled on Sam in raging disbelief. "I can't believe you contacted my father, after all I confided in you!" she stormed.

"It was precisely *because* of what you told me that I called him," Sam said.

Nora glared at Sam, her face alternately going white and red. She was so embarrassed and humiliated she wanted to die. "I see." She regarded Sam icily, then, unable to prevent herself, taunted him sarcastically, "Still part social worker, part sheriff, right, Sam?"

Sam frowned. "Your father was half out of his mind with worry," Sam explained curtly, his expression stony with resolve. "It was cruel to let him continue to agonize."

"But it was all right to hurt me, is that it?" Nora cried, incensed.

Abruptly Sam looked as though he felt as miserable as Nora did. "Look, I asked your father not to come here until you were ready to talk to him. I hoped that would be soon, but in any case, I implored him to give you as much time to sort things out as you needed."

"I couldn't do that, either," Charles Kingsley interjected. "What if she had run away again before we had a chance to speak?"

"I do not believe this," Nora muttered, raking both her hands through her hair.

"What's going on?" Gus asked, sauntering up to join the group.

"I'll tell you what's going on. Once a dupe, always a dupe," Nora muttered. She stormed toward the exit, bypassing the coat check and sweeping out onto the street. Her head held high, she stalked, shivering, past the helicopter that had set down in the empty Whittakers parking lot.

Right behind her, Sam and her father both followed, hard on her heels.

Seeing that she was shivering, Sam tore off his tuxedo jacket and threw it around her shoulders. Nora shrugged it off and tossed it right back in his face. "You've helped me enough, Sam."

Sam put both hands on her shoulders and spun her around. Once again, his tuxedo jacket, still warm with the heat of his body and scented with his cologne, was slid over her shoulders. Keeping a firm grip on her all the while, Sam stared down at her. "Dammit, Nora, your father's come all this way. Hear him out!"

Nora noticed that Sam hadn't mentioned anything about Geoff. And where was Geoff, by the way? Why hadn't he come out here, too? "*You* hear him out," Nora told Sam. She bent her knees, and ducked away from his grip.

"Where are you going?" Sam demanded, thoroughly exasperated.

Nora tossed her head and, deciding she was much warmer with Sam's jacket than without it, closed it more tightly around her body. Both men could freeze, as far as she was concerned. "I don't much care, as long as it is far away from you and my father as possible!"

"Nora," Sam warned, "do not cross that street."

"Watch me," Nora countered, swiftly noting the absence of traffic. Ignoring the red traffic light and the Do Not Walk sign, she bypassed the crosswalk and headed across the street at an angle.

"All right, you've given me no choice." Sam overtook her easily and clamped a hand on her wrist. "You're under arrest."

Nora's jaw dropped. She whirled to face Sam. "What!"

"For jaywalking," Sam continued.

Nora rolled her eyes. "This is ridiculous."

"I agree," Sam said sagely. "You're old enough to know better, Nora—about a lot of things."

The double entendre was not lost on her. He was talking about their romance and her father, too.

She was not about to let him lay a guilt trip on her, after what he'd done. "*You* are making a fool of yourself, Sam Whittaker," she told him sternly.

His eyes glittering dangerously, he stared down at her. "So are you," he said, very, very softly.

Nora's pulse picked up as she became even more aware of the warm, implacable grip he held on her wrist. She drew a deep breath and spoke in clear, concise tones. "Sam Whittaker, if you take me over to that jail, I swear you are going to regret it."

In return, Sam gave her a taunting half smile that didn't begin to reach his eyes. "If I don't take you over there, I'll regret it, too, so it looks like I'm damned if I do and damned if I don't."

At long last, Nora's father, who had been watching the entire exchange with an air of absolute amazement, interjected, "Listen here, Sam. Nora. If I may say a word—"

"No!" Sam and Nora said in unison.

His own irritation mounting swiftly, Charles Kingsley headed across Main Street at the angle Nora and Sam had already taken. "I resent that!" Charles shouted.

"And I object to the way you just jaywalked," Sam said, taking hold of Charles's arm. "You're under arrest, too, sir."

Nora laughed bitterly even as Sam commandeered her and her father into the sheriff's office. "Really, Sam," she said in a low, mocking tone, hanging on to her dignity with effort. "This is going too far, even for you!"

"I'd have to agree," Charles repeated, quite calmly.

"Nora and I can talk without you putting us in jail on some trumped-up traffic charge."

"Given Nora's penchant for running away from her problems, and the people who've hurt her, without giving anyone a chance to resolve anything?" Sam drawled with a knowing look in her direction. "I wouldn't bet on those odds, sir, and neither should you."

Undeterred in his mission, Sam held on to Nora's elbow with one hand, and unlocked the jail cell with the other. "You first, sir. Nora." He shut them both in and locked the door.

"And I thought I despised you before," Nora told him, shooting daggers at him with her eyes.

Sam rubbed a hand along his jaw and regarded them both stoically for a long moment before he began to talk in a low, mesmerizing tone. "Right up until the time of my parents' death two years ago, I never worried about a harsh word or missed opportunity, because I thought we had all the time in the world to be together."

Sam swallowed hard and went on in a voice roughened with pain and grief. "Not a day goes by that I don't miss them or regret the things we were never blessed with the time to say or do. You two, on the other hand, are lucky," he continued sternly. "You may have lost a wife, sir." Sam gave Charles a hard look, and followed that with a daunting glance at Nora. "And Nora, you may have lost a mother. But you *still* have each other.

"So yes, even if you hate me for it, Nora, I'm giving you a chance to work things out with your dad, and vice versa." Sam paused meaningfully, allowing his words to sink in, before he shrugged. "What you two do with that chance is up to you."

Chapter Thirteen

Nora glared at her father as Sam left the two of them alone and walked back to the outer office. Charles regarded her with a mixture of fatherly patience and contrition.

Having to work to keep her anger both intact and in check, Nora folded her arms in front of her. "You want to give me an explanation, Daddy?" she said hotly as the family showdown began. "Well, here's your chance, and while we're at it, let's start with my losing my job in New York City."

Charles looked at her as if to suggest she was getting hysterical over nothing. "I admit I pulled a few strings to see your position with Leland and Brooks was eliminated."

Fighting for patience, Nora closed her eyes and counted to ten. "Why would you do such a thing?" she asked quietly, after she opened her eyes once again.

Charles shrugged, as if his actions had been unavoidable. "Because you didn't seem all that happy with your life in New York City, and you refused to even discuss coming back to Pittsburgh to live."

Nora didn't deny that she had stayed at L and B long after she realized the New York City advertising world was not for her, in order to prove that she had deserved to be hired by the company all along, even without her father's incessant string-pulling.

Nora released an exasperated sigh and, so tired of fighting she wanted to die, sank down on one of the two cell cots. "Daddy, I told you a million times I'm not cut out for the restaurant business—it just doesn't captivate me the way it does you and Geoff." She knew they burned to have Hamburger Heaven right up there in the leagues of McDonald's and Burger King, but for her, the desire just wasn't there.

Charles nodded knowingly. Hitching up his trousers, he sat on the cot on the other side of the cell. "Which is exactly why I gave Geoff shares in the company as a wedding present," Charles explained, as if it were the most rational thing in the world.

"Without telling me?" Nora reminded him, still aghast over that little secret.

Charles shrugged. He leaned forward, clasped hands between his knees. "I figured you'd think I was trying to buy Geoff and you'd object if I told you my plans. And I was right. You're furious." He paused. "How did you find out, anyway?"

"I saw you and Geoff signing the prenup, which brings me to the next point, Daddy. A prenuptial agreement, when there is one, is supposed to be between a bride and groom, not the groom and his father-in-law."

Charles fixed her with an inquiring look. "Would

you have signed one with Geoff if I asked you to do so?''

"No," Nora shot back stubbornly. "Nor would I have given him shares in the company equal to mine. I expected Geoff to marry me because he loved me and wanted to build a life with me. I expected us to live on our salaries, not my inheritance."

Charles sighed. "I was just trying to ensure your marriage got off to a good start. And whether you believe it or not, Geoff cares about you as much as I do."

Without warning, Geoff walked in, carrying all three of their winter coats. Sam had not come in with him.

Nora frowned as Geoff, picking up on the last of her conversation with Charles, added, "I just wanted you to be happy, Nora. Your dad convinced me this was the way."

Nora looked at Geoff, standing on the other side of the bars. She did believe he cared about her, but as a friend, not a potential lover, wife and lifelong partner.

Furthermore, for someone who had been her friend since elementary school, he had shown a disturbing lack of understanding about what it took to make her happy in a marriage. Which was, she supposed, yet another sign that they were not, and had never been, meant to be together.

"Well, it's not the way to make me happy, Geoff." Nora turned back to Charles. Even if Geoff hadn't known better, surely Charles had. She had the distinct feeling that there had been an ulterior motive to this.

"What were you thinking?" she demanded of her father hotly.

Charles shrugged. "That Geoff owning part of the business would bring us closer together, as a family, in a way we haven't really been since your mother died." Charles paused. "You know how active your mother was in helping me build this business. Her input was invaluable. Working together was a very satisfying experience for us. I hoped the same would happen for you and Geoff, and that you might become more interested in your inheritance if your husband was involved and it was more of a family affair for all of us. Besides, you know Geoff's always been like a son to me. He's been working with me ever since the two of you graduated from college. With you two tying the knot, it seemed natural to involve him in the company in a more fundamental way."

Nora shook her head in exasperation, her anger fading as she realized her father's heart had been in the right place, even if his actions had been totally misguided. "Daddy, we can be close without working together, just by being honest with each other. As for the business. If you want to take Geoff in as a partner, then do so, and do it with my blessing. But don't ask him to marry me so that you can officially bring him into the family, because it's not fair to any of us."

Still looking a little sheepish, Geoff set the coats down on a chair located next to the door and stuck his hands in the pockets of his trousers. "Does this mean our wedding is off?" he asked Nora, looking as if he already knew—and had accepted—the answer to that.

"It has to be," Nora said gently, her anger fading as she recalled the years they'd been friends. "We're not in love with each other, Geoff. Not the way we should be, because if we were, you never would've been able to keep such a secret from me."

Nora saw the regret etched on Geoff's face and knew he had never meant to hurt her. He had been maneuvered into behaving this way by her well-meaning but totally out-of-line father, the same way she had been. Hence, she knew it wasn't fair to lay all the blame on Geoff or her dad. Not when they'd all been searching for happiness and trying to do what was best for each other and the "family" as a whole. And her Dad had been right—she had been unhappy in New York City, for reasons that were only partly related to her dissatisfaction with big-city life and her high-pressure job at L and B. And even more to the increasing emptiness in her personal life.

Nora sighed and stood. "To be honest, Geoff, I was having doubts about marrying you before the ceremony, anyway. I was in a panic, because I knew in my heart it wasn't right. We didn't love each other enough, or even in the way that we should, to get married. So you going over those papers with my father before the ceremony actually worked in our favor, because it gave me the push I needed to call the whole thing off at the last second. Otherwise, with a church full of people and the potential for humiliation, I doubt I'd have had the nerve."

Geoff looked at her through the bars. "Can we be friends again? I'd hate to lose that, too."

Nora stepped forward and linked hands with him. "I don't want to lose our friendship, either, Geoff."

"Good." Geoff breathed a sigh of relief. "And, Nora? I'm sorry I hurt you."

"Me too," Nora said softly, giving Geoff's hand a final squeeze before releasing it.

She turned to Charles. "As for you," she said sternly, "you've got to stop meddling in my life, because I'm telling you right now, I've absolutely had it with your overbearing manner."

Charles stood. "I understand," he said contritely. "And you're completely right."

"Thank you."

"Therefore, if you want me to make a few calls so you can get your job at L and B back..." Charles offered optimistically as he closed the distance between them.

Nora rolled her eyes; there he went again. "First, if L and B could fire me on your whim, they're not the company for me, anyway. Second, you've got to stop interfering, even when you think it's in my best interest, and start listening to me. *Really listening*, Daddy."

Charles nodded and engulfed Nora in an awkward but nevertheless very soothing and emotional hug. "I promise I will," he said thickly. He drew back. "And you promise me something, too, sweetheart."

"What?" Nora said, aware that her eyes were misting with unexpected tears.

"That you won't run away ever again," Charles said, his voice breaking. "Because Sam Whittaker was right—I really was half out of my mind with worry.'' Charles paused as tears glistened in his eyes. ''I couldn't bear it if anything ever happened to you,'' he said softly. ''So promise me—''

''I promise,'' Nora said, crying now openly, too.

''I think this is my cue to leave,'' Geoff said on a delicate cough as he wiped his eyes. ''I think I'll go out and talk to the sheriff again, and see if I can't get you two released.''

Charles waved off the offer. ''Don't hurry it along too much,'' he told Geoff happily. ''This is the most intimate discussion Nora and I've had in years.''

Nora shook her head at her dad and laughed softly. ''You're incorrigible,'' she scolded affectionately. ''Geoff, find that oh-so-controlling Sheriff Whittaker and get us out of here.''

''Will do.'' Geoff picked up his winter coat and headed, whistling, back down the corridor toward the front of the building.

''Now, about jobs,'' Charles asked. ''If not something at L and B or Hamburger Haven, what would you like to do?''

Nora smiled. She patted the cot. ''Sit down, Daddy and I'll tell you about it.''

''SO HOW'S IT GOING in there?'' Sam asked Geoff when he came back out.

''Nora forgave me. Our marriage is still off. She's relieved. And now that I think about it,'' Geoff said, heaving an enormous sigh, ''I am, too.''

''What about her dad?'' Sam asked, knowing that the hurt of that betrayal had gone much deeper.

Geoff smiled. ''She's forgiven Charles, too.''

"Good." Sam wanted Nora to be happy more than anything in the world. Geoff could not make her happy. Sam knew that, given half a chance, he could. The trick would be convincing Nora. Given her resistance to being tricked or bullied into anything, she had to be mighty ticked off at him for arresting her on trumped-up charges and locking her in that jail cell with her father.

"I'd give them a few more minutes, then go in and see about letting her dad go," Geoff advised.

"Not Nora, too?"

Geoff paused. "I've known Nora a long time, since we were kids. I've never seen her look at anyone the way she was looking at you. If I were you, I wouldn't let that go lightly."

Sam smiled. "I don't intend to."

"Good." Geoff shook Sam's hand. "I have a feeling the two of us are going to see each other around."

"Let's hope so," Sam said as he walked Geoff out.

Unfortunately, he wasn't as sure about that as he would've liked. The truth was, because he figured he had only until the snowstorm ended to make Nora his, he had allowed his relationship with Nora to take on the momentum of a runaway train going down a mountainside. And he'd done that knowing she was angry and emotional and running away. He had done it knowing she was vulnerable and uncertain, after the abrupt cancellation of her wedding, the loss of her job and all she had believed in and counted on in the past. Yet he had wanted her so desperately, he had been so sure they were right for each other, that he had staked his claim on her anyway.

At the time, she'd been too caught up in the passion of the moment, the heady freedom of running away and the time-stands-still feeling of the blizzard to think much beyond the moment or what the two of them had been feeling for each other.

Now, the snowstorm of the century was over. The outside world was already closing in on them. And she'd apparently made up with her father, and made peace with her ex-fiancé. Would she want to go home to Pittsburgh again? Would she chalk their brief affair up as a mistake? And if so, what would he do? Let her know she was breaking his heart and crushing his hopes? Continue to put the full-court press on her? Or be gallant and understanding and let her go?

"I'M DYING to know what's happening in here," Kimberlee said moments later, as she and Gus swept into the sheriff's office.

"So am I, but that's not why we came over here, remember, little sis?" Gus said, poking Kimberlee in the ribs. "You had something to tell Sam, remember?"

Kimberlee flushed self-consciously. "Oh, yeah. I got out my college profile books this morning, before you got back to town, and I looked up all the nursing programs in the Chicago vicinity. I've still got time to apply to three of them, so I'm doing that right away. Second, if I don't get in, I'll go to college here in West Virginia for a year, and consider transferring after that. And in the meantime, Gus will spot me money for airline tickets, as long as I keep my grades up, so I can come and visit all of you once a month if I'm going to school in Chicago, or go see Kenny once a month in Chicago, if I end up going to school here. However, it has to work out so I can see Kenny more than I'm seeing him now, *and* be with the family here on a regular basis, and still pursue my own career goals, too."

"Granddad and Gran both think love is too precious to be squandered, and I've got to say, now my heart's been taken, I agree," Gus said. "But you're the guardian, so you have to agree."

"I agree," Sam said softly, impressed with the change in his little sister's attitude. "What changed your mind?"

"It was just everything you and Nora and everyone has been saying. Plus the fact you were right about the sledding incident—someone could have been really hurt, and for what, so my friends and I could all act like rebels without a clue? There are better ways to seek a little freedom and independence."

Sam grinned. "I'll second that."

"Anyway," Kimberlee continued earnestly, suddenly looking much older than her seventeen years, "I knew all along that I needed to have my own life, as well as my own love life, but it took me a while to admit I was never going to pout my way to maturity." Kimberlee hugged Sam, hard. "I'm sorry I've been giving you such a hard time," she said in a low, choked voice.

"I'm sorry we've been fighting, too," Sam said thickly, hugging her back with all his might. "I know I don't handle things anywhere near as well as Mom and Dad did, but you have to know that the bottom line is, I only want what's best for you.''

Kimberlee nodded. Clearly, she was as choked up—and happy to be done with their fighting—as he was. "And I want that for you, too. Speaking of which—" Kimberlee paused dramatically as she reached for a tissue to wipe the tears from her face "—where's Nora?"

Gus looked at Sam. "There are rumors floating around the reception that you arrested her."

Sam shrugged, and Gus rolled his eyes and swore when he realized it was so. "You're in trouble now, little bro," he conceded, with a playful punch at Sam's shoulder. "That is *not* how you romance women in this day and age."

"Tell me about it," Sam drawled. But what choice did he have, with Nora running away yet again? Whether she liked it or not, he had known she had to face her father and Geoff and at least try to work things out. And now that that was apparently happening, it changed everything. It took away Nora's need to be there in Clover Creek, instead of Pittsburgh. It took away her need to get involved with a man not selected for her by her father. Like it or not, the blizzard that had brought them together was ending, and that left him feeling very uncertain about what was going to happen next.

"You're not thinking Nora's in any way like Susan, are you?" Gus said.

Sam didn't know what to say that. He only knew he had been very deeply disappointed by a woman once, when she refused to admit she was wrong in behaving the way she had; she'd chosen her career advancement over her relationship with him, rather than change her self-destructive ways. He didn't want to be hurt like that again. And he was aware that it could happen. Nora could decide to leave Clover Creek, and her relationship with him, behind for so many reasons, the least of which was that it had all happened very fast. She could refuse to forgive him for the manipulative things he had done to help reconcile her with her father.

And in a sense, she was right. He was the sheriff here, not a social worker....

"You *are* going to ask Nora to stay now that it's stopped snowing, aren't you?" Kimberlee said earnestly. "At least until your romance with her has more of a chance to get off the ground and she finishes designing the new ads and store slogan for Granddad and Gran?"

"In these days of telecommuting, Nora can do that from anywhere," Sam conceded reluctantly, though he was certain Nora would honor the commitment she'd made to his grandparents. "As for where she is when she does that work, ultimately, the choice is Nora's." And the same was true of their romance.

The gallant thing to do would be to let her decide where she wanted to be, and with whom, without undue pressure from him—even if doing so tore him apart, heart and soul. And if, heaven help them both, that was Pittsburgh...instead of Clover Creek... And Sam had to admit that careerwise, Pittsburgh had a lot more to offer than Clover Creek. If she decided he was too "small-town" for her, too "do-gooding" and "interfering," then he was just going to have to deal with it. And not give her anything more—like hurt, angry words between them—to regret.

Gus looked at Sam and seemed to read his mind.

"I'd still give it all you've got in convincing her to stay," Gus advised sagely. "Even if it means doing something drastic. Otherwise, Kimberlee and I both have a hunch you're going to be regretting it for a very long time."

Chapter Fourteen

Half an hour later, Nora and her dad had hashed out everything that needed hashing out and she was about to start banging on the cell bars, demanding to be released, when Sam sauntered in. Though he'd long ago dispensed with his black bow tie, he was still in the tuxedo pants and shirt he had worn to Gus's wedding. Her heart sped up at the sight of him, and her stomach fluttered with a thousand butterflies. But she knew she had every right to be ticked off at him, and she was not going to let him think he could get away with interfering in her life this way.

"You think I'm going to forgive you for this, don't you?" Nora said coolly, the depth and breadth of her anger sending her emotions into high gear.

"I came in here thinking the answer to that would be an unequivocal yes," Sam remarked with a roguish smile as he eyed her determinedly.

Nora folded her arms in front of her and watched mutely as he unlocked the cell door, swung the door open and stepped inside.

"But, after taking one look at your face," he drawled, his eyes searching hers with laser accuracy,

"I think I'll amend my answer to 'A guy can dream, can't he?'"

"Very funny." Nora situated herself at the back of the cell, as far away from his unnervingly masculine presence as possible. She continued to regard him cantankerously, knowing her pique was her best defense. "And for the record, I am not—I repeat, *not*—forgiving you for this," she continued stonily.

"Not even if I tell you the charges of jaywalking were dropped on account of stupidity on the part of the sheriff?" Sam said wryly as he held the cell door open and gestured for Charles to depart.

"Not even then," Nora said huffily. "And you know why? Because you betrayed me on the worst possible level, and you did it by high-handedly manipulating events so that I had no choice but to make up with my father. Not on my own timetable, as it should have been, by all rights, but on yours."

Charles intervened. "Nora—"

"Daddy, you stay out of this! This is strictly between Sam and me!"

Her father backed up and stepped outside the cell. "You're right. It's your life. Your decision. Sorry, Sam." Charles gave Sam a penitent look. "I'd like to help, but in this instance my hands are tied by a promise I made my daughter—a promise I fully intend to keep. There will be no more interfering on my part."

"I understand, sir," Sam replied. He gave Nora a speculative look and stepped toward her, deliberately invading her space. "And your daughter's right," Sam continued smoothly, keeping his eyes locked on her face. "This sticky situation does belong strictly to us."

Uh-oh. Nora knew that look. That look meant trouble. Nora backed up until the backs of her knees touched the edge of the iron cot. "What are you thinking?" Nora demanded, picking up on the glint in his eyes.

Sam shrugged. "That Gus and Kimberlee are right. If I don't do something drastic to keep you here with me, you might walk out of my life, never to return again. And I don't want that to happen, Nora. So..." Sam pulled the door shut behind him with a resounding clang that set her heart to pounding all the harder. "I guess I'm going to have to do something to make sure you don't run away from me. At least not until you and I have a chance to talk."

Nora stared at Sam, unable to believe his audacity, as he locked the door behind him, removed the key and dropped it into his pants pocket. She turned to her father. If ever she'd needed his help, it was now. But strangely, Charles was motionless. And, worse, looking rather pleased with the whole situation, and her new beau. "Daddy! You're *not* going to let him get away with this, are you?" Nora demanded, incensed.

To Nora's mounting frustration, her father lifted both his hands in surrender. "I'm staying out of it, remember, honey?" Charles traded amused glances with Sam. "Guess I'll see you in the morning," Charles said as he headed jauntily down the corridor. "I've got to go find Geoff."

The door to the outer office shut softly behind him.

Nora turned back to Sam. For the first time since that morning, the two of them were really, truly alone. As always, the sexual electricity crackled between them, as vibrant and dangerous and hot as any winter fire. And Sam Whittaker, damn his treacherous soul, did not appear to mind that fact one bit!

Looking as if he were enjoying every delicious moment of tension between them, Sam kicked off his shoes, stretched out on the cot and folded his hands behind his head.

Nora drew what was left of her pride around her like an invisible force field. She didn't care how sexy Sam Whittaker was, or how much passion he stirred up inside her. Darn it all, she was not going to fall victim to a meddling, controlling, overprotective man again! "Now what are you doing?" Nora demanded.

"I'm getting comfortable," Sam replied, with a determination that had her pulse jumping. "I think it's going to be a long wait for that temper of yours to cool down enough for us to be able to talk in a reasonable manner, so I advise you to kick off your shoes and do the same."

Nora stomped closer, her high heels clicking on the concrete floor. She removed the tuxedo jacket she'd drawn about her shoulders and let it flutter onto his abdomen. "This is not funny, Sam."

"I agree." He left the jacket where it lay and nodded at her, still regarding her with predatory grace. "It's not."

Nora drew a deep breath. Now that she had finally given him back his jacket, she was cold again, in a way only his arms would warm. "I want out of this cell."

Sam's laugh was low and wicked and determinedly male as he flashed her a wolfish grin. He tossed his jacket aside and patted his pants pocket. "You know where the key is."

Nora did an about-face, and marched away from him until she stood against the opposite wall. Pivoting around to face him again, she leaned back against the pale green cinder-block wall and folded her arms tightly beneath her breasts. "I don't care how long we stay in here. I'm not coming over there," she announced with a defiant toss of her head.

Sam shrugged his broad shoulders and rolled onto his side. "Have it your own way."

"You are stubborn as a mule," Nora fumed, as she began to pace back and forth in irritation.

"I'm stubborn!" Sam echoed incredulously, arrowing a thumb at his chest. He vaulted to a sitting position on the metal cot, leaned forward urgently. "Let me ask you something," he said as he got slowly, deliberately, to his feet. "Do you always want to be right, or do you want to be happy?" He strode forward, closing the distance between them in two quick strides. "'Cause the way I see it, we've both made mistakes here." Hands cupping her shoulders warmly, he held her in front of him, and continued passionately, "I never should've called your dad without your permission, and you never should've interfered with the workings of this sheriff's department by intercepting those messages, or accused me of wanting you only for the reward money, 'cause I know you know in your heart it's not true.''

He pulled her closer, so that they were touching, in one long warmth-inducing line. "I want you, all right, but I want you for you," he confessed with gruff honesty.

He studied her bleakly, a muscle working in his cheek. "The question is, are you going to hang on to your grudges, which are only bound to get worse with time, or are you going to get in there and roll up your sleeves and get to work to fix what's wrong with us? Because I can't do it alone, Nora," Sam confided ruefully. He released her abruptly and stepped back. "No one can. All relationships are two-way streets. All relationships require people to grow and change and own up to their mistakes."

He paused, his eyes gleaming moistly, as the tense seconds drew out between them. "The bottom line is, do you have it in your heart to forgive me?" Sam queried bluntly as he reached into his pocket, removed the key to the cell and folded it ever so gently into her palm. He swallowed hard, and his voice dropped another devastating notch. "Or are you going to keep on running away?"

"That was quite a speech," Nora said in a low, trembling voice.

"I know," Sam replied with mock gravity as he cupped her chin between his thumb and forefinger and turned her face to his. Without giving her a chance to say anything, he lowered his lips to hers and delivered a slow, devastatingly thorough kiss that told her volumes about the passion he felt for her, and perhaps always would, and nothing of what was in his heart.

He tangled one hand in the softness of her hair and rubbed the other palm possessively down her spine. "I had an hour or so to perfect it while you were talking with your father."

Nora recalled Sam's words to her before he'd left her alone with her father. ...*I thought we had all the time in the world to be together. Not a day goes by that I don't miss them or regret the things we never had time to say and do.*

That was the way she felt about her and Sam. But the bottom line was, though he'd indicated he wanted to be with her in the physical sense, he hadn't said he loved her yet. And without love, Nora knew, it was not realistic to believe they'd ever make it over the long haul.

She cared too much about Sam to want to hurt him, and she was too practical to want to hurt herself.

"There were also a ton of questions in there," Nora continued, knowing they had one more very important bridge to cross. She linked hands with Sam and held on tight, hoping with all her might things would turn out right. "I guess I should answer some of them."

He looked down at their hands and tightened his grip on her fingers. "That would be nice, I agree."

Nora tilted her face up to his and kept her eyes on his. "You're right," she murmured contritely. "We both have made mistakes. And I have been running away from my problems up till now. It's time that stopped. But as for me staying here or us rolling up our sleeves to work on our problems, I have to ask you, Sam, is simple desire and maybe even friendship enough to make this relationship of ours work the way we both want and need it to work to be happy?''

A mixture of disappointment and displeasure gleamed in Sam's golden-brown eyes. ''You're comparing us to you and Geoff, aren't you?''

One of them had to be sensible, and Nora loved Sam too much to give him less than he deserved. ''Geoff and I tried to base our relationship on a friendship that went way back. Even if he had been honest with me about the prenup, even if he hadn't worked for my father, it still never would've worked.'' And the last thing she wanted was to enter into another engagement for all the wrong reasons.

Sam's lips tightened. ''You said it yourself—you didn't have passion with Geoff.''

''True,'' Nora acknowledged slowly. ''But I'm not sure passion or friendship is enough to build an enduring relationship on, never mind a marriage, and that is where we've both said we want to go, isn't it, Sam? To the point in our lives where we can marry the person we love and settle down and have a home and family with them?''

Sam's expression turned gruff, unrelenting. ''I don't deny that's where I want to be.'' He was silent a moment, the uncertainty he felt showing on his face. He appeared to be weighing all the options, just as he did when confronted with some of the more difficult situations he ran into on the job. Nora hated to think that she was just another problem he faced, but it was possible, and she needed to be realistic here, for both their sakes.

"Is it only the lack of true love between us holding you back, or is it something else, too?" he asked eventually. "Like the fact you're still looking for work in your field and I live in a very small town?"

Her heart pounding, Nora shook her head. "I love Clover Creek, and there are a ton of job opportunities here. Quite frankly, I would view starting my own advertising agency here as a challenge."

Briefly Sam seemed to hearten, but his next question was laced with wariness. "How would your father feel about that?"

Nora sighed. "I think he finally understands, as much as I love him and want to be close to him, it's also time I made my own way in the world, apart from his influence and connections."

"Then what's holding you back?" Sam asked casually.

You, Sam, Nora thought. *And the words and feelings you haven't expressed and might not even have for me.*

Keeping her emotions in check with effort, Nora shrugged and, disengaging her hand from his, turned away from his probing gaze. "You've said it yourself. Clover Creek is a small town. I'm not sure how a long-term love affair would go over here."

Sam sighed and smoothed a hand through his hair. Pragmatic as ever, he replied, "Probably not well, if you want to know the truth. That's why we'd have to get married if we're going to be together." He paused and shrugged his broad shoulders apologetically. "It may sound old-fashioned, but I've got an example to set for my sister and the kids here. And I wouldn't want to do anything that would hurt or embarrass my grandparents.''

He still hadn't said anything about love! For all she knew, he was still regarding her as one of the part law enforcement, part social work cases he dealt with on a daily basis.

''And then there are children,'' Sam continued sensibly, settling back on the cot. Taking her wrist in hand, he guided her onto his lap. ''We've both said we want them. For that reason alone, we should be married.''

He was trying to get what he wanted out of life and problem-solve for her at the same time. And while she admired his deeply ingrained gallantry, it still wasn't enough. ''I've disappointed you again, haven't I?'' Sam guessed softly, turning her to face him as a world-weary light came into his eyes.

Nora shrugged. Aware that she was treacherously close to tears, she allowed stubbornly, ''I just don't think any of what you've just cited is reason enough to make a lifelong commitment on.''

''Then what is?'' Sam studied her. Recognition dawned in his eyes. ''Wait a minute.'' He tugged her against him. ''You're not hesitating because you're uncertain of my feelings for you, are you?''

Nora flushed. As difficult as it was, it was time to put all their cards on the table. ''Look, I know you feel guilty about what happened between us, the fact I had never been intimate with a man before. You indicated as much at the time. I know you're Mr.

Responsibility personified, and I also know you desire me, on a daily, hourly basis, at least for the moment, but—''

Sam pressed a silencing finger against her lips and interrupted gruffly, ''Wait just a doggone minute here. I readily admit I wish I'd known about your lack of experience ahead of time, but what I feel for you now has nothing to do with guilt over what happened or any misguided responsibility on my part. And furthermore, I don't just desire you or like you or have fun with you. I love you, Nora, heart and soul.''

Nora's heart soared as all her dreams came true. ''Then why didn't you say so?'' she whispered, as tears of joy filled her eyes, and relief flowed through her in great calming waves.

''Because I thought you knew!'' Sam replied hoarsely as he gently stroked her face. ''And because I didn't want to pressure you. You had enough, coming from your dad. I thought it might be too soon to be talking about all this, coming on the heels of your almost-marriage to Geoff.'' He studied her upturned face, shook his head and grinned again. ''Guess not.''

Nora wreathed her arms around Sam and held him tight, the warm strength of him a balm to her soul. ''Geoff was never in the running for love of my life, Sam. You are. And for the record—'' she drew back to kiss him tenderly, putting everything she felt into a gentle, lingering kiss ''—I love you, too, heart and soul.''

Sam kissed her until she was dizzy with desire, warm with love, and full of hope. ''So what do you think, Nora?'' he teased, as he began to kiss his way down her neck. ''Long engagement or short?''

Nora cupped his face with her hands and kissed him back soundly. ''Do you even have to ask?''

ONE MONTH LATER, the snow was gone, the sun was shining. And all their family and friends from Pittsburgh, New York City, Chicago and Clover Creek were gathered round as Sam and Nora recited their wedding vows. When they'd finished, there wasn't a dry eye or an empty heart in the merrily assembled group.

''So, where's the honeymoon going to be?'' Gus said, ambling forward, Evelyn by his side.

''You'll have to ask Sam that,'' Nora said, leaning against Sam and savoring the warmth and strength and essence that was him. ''All I know is that it's a surprise.''

Sam winked. ''A groom has to have some secrets.''

Nora wrapped her arms around Sam's waist and leaned in close. ''So does the bride,'' she quipped. And she had some lingerie in her suitcase that was guaranteed to heat his blood and make the days and nights ahead memorable for both of them.

''Uh-oh, buddy,'' Gus teased, elbowing his brother in the ribs. ''Sounds like you're going to have your hands full!''

Sam grinned mischievously as he bent to kiss Nora. ''I'm counting on it.''

Hours later, replete with food and champagne and newly-wedded bliss, Sam carried Nora into the honeymoon suite at the Mountain View lodge.

"And now for the part I like best," Nora teased, taking in the view of the snowcapped Allegheny Mountains.

Sam set her down gently on the bed and reached into his suitcase. "Not quite yet. First, I have a gift for you."

He brought out a beribboned gift, then went over to draw the drapes as Nora opened the box with trembling hands. "It's a lease!" she exclaimed in surprise.

Sam grinned and sank down next to her on the bed. "For that office space you've had your eye on, for your new advertising agency in Clover Creek. The lease agreement includes utilities and is paid up for a full year, in advance." He covered her hand with his. "Once we get some office equipment in there for you, you'll be all set."

"Oh, Sam—" It meant so much to her to have his support.

"You like it?"

"Very much." Nora wreathed her hands around his neck and kissed him deeply. She drew back slowly, holding his eyes. "And speaking of presents," she said softly, "I have a gift for you, too." She took his hand and put it on her tummy and knew instantly from the oh-so-willing but slightly befuddled expression on his face that Sam clearly hadn't a clue what she was trying to tell him.

"It's a baby, silly," Nora teased softly. "A by-product of those two nights and one day we were snowed in at your place."

Sam broke out into a broad grin. "You're kidding."

"Nope. According to Doc Ellen, it's a done deal. This time next winter, we'll be rocking a cradle."

Sam kissed her again and gently stroked her hair. "Sounds like we really have a lot to celebrate tonight."

Nora nodded. "But first, some music, maestro," she said, reaching over to turn on the FM radio beside the bed.

Instead of the romantic music they expected, a weather bulletin was being broadcast. "...absolutely unbelievable," the announcer was saying excitedly. "For another record blizzard to be hitting the entire East Coast just weeks after the first.... This is turning out to be some winter!"

"He's right about that," Nora murmured happily as Sam and she snuggled together on the bed.

"It should start snowing in West Virginia in another couple of hours...." the announcer continued.

"Well," Nora said playfully as she began slowly and sensually unbuttoning the buttons on Sam's shirt. "If we're going to be stuck somewhere, it sure looks like we're in the right place."

Sam undid her zipper and gathered her close enough to leave a string of kisses down her throat. "I couldn't think of anywhere I'd rather be," he murmured, sliding a warm palm over her skin. They kissed soulfully, until both of them were trembling all over. They drew apart shakily, both of them knowing where they wanted this to lead, as static crackled, the weather bulletin ended and soft, romantic music resumed playing on the radio.

Together, they undressed. Drawing on all the

power and wonder of their love, they held each other's eyes and slipped beneath the sheets.

"At last, we both have everything we ever wanted," Sam murmured, as he framed Nora's face and kissed her gently.

Contentment and wonder shuddered through Nora as she thought about their life together and the love they shared. And she knew their future had never been brighter. "And then some," she agreed.

**Make a Valentine's date
for the premiere of**

⬥ HARLEQUIN® **Movies**

starting February 14, 1998 with

Debbie Macomber's

This Matter of Marriage

on **the movie channel** tmc

Just tune in to **The Movie Channel** the **second Saturday night** of every month at 9:00 p.m. EST to join us, and be swept away by the sheer thrill of romance brought to life. Watch for details of upcoming movies—in books, in your television viewing guide and in stores.

If you are not currently a subscriber to The Movie Channel, simply call your local cable or satellite provider for more details. Call today, and don't miss out on the romance!

the movie channel tmc
*100% pure movies.
100% pure fun.*

⬥ HARLEQUIN®
Makes any time special.™

**Cupid's going undercover
this Valentine's Day in**

The Cupid Connection

**Cupid has his work
cut out for him this
Valentine's Day with these
three stories about three
couples who are just too *busy*
to fall in love...well, not for long!**

ONE MORE VALENTINE
by Anne Stuart
BE MINE, VALENTINE
by Vicki Lewis Thompson
BABY ON THE DOORSTEP
by Kathy Gillen Thacker

Make the Cupid Connection this February 1998!

Available wherever Harlequin and Silhouette books are sold.

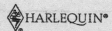 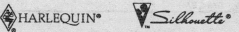

HARLEQUIN® Silhouette®

Look us up on-line at: http://www.romance.net   HREQ298

Don't miss these Harlequin favorites by some of our top-selling authors!

HBLJM98